I0555887

Children of the Wolf

Children of the Wild, Volume 2

Prudence MacLeod

Published by Prudence MacLeod, 2024.

Shapeshifter

by

Prudence MacLeod

Copyright, September 2015

Second edition.

(Formerly titled Children of the Wolf.)

CHILDREN OF THE WOLF

First edition. February 19, 2024.

Copyright © 2024 Prudence MacLeod.

ISBN: 978-1927478615

Written by Prudence MacLeod.

Cornering a Killer

CURSING SOFTLY, AND wishing for a fur coat as she trudged through the snow in human form, the vampire shivered. Ah, to hell with it, she stripped off her clothes and buried them in the snow before changing her form into the sabre-toothed tiger; the cat could track the maddened killer more easily, and she had a fur coat.

THE TALL WOMAN TRUDGED along behind the three men, stepping in their tracks to make travel through the snow easier. The cold wind was blocked somewhat by the trees, but she was aware of its bite on her face. Immediately in front of her walked the burly form of her boss and buddy, Agent Sawchuk. For the past number of years they and their team had worked the tougher cases together, dealing with that which no other agency could handle. Working for the vampire king was much the same.

To the front of the small procession walked two of the local deputies, a couple of good old boys. They carried their heavy hunting rifles at the ready as they watched the trail before them. Suddenly they stopped, confused. The taller of the two men spoke softly. "Agent Sawchuk, look at this. Your tracker's footprints stop here. Her backpack is there. It looks like she was taken by a big cat."

"A really big cat, Sam," said the other deputy. "I've never seen cat tracks like that. These tracks are way too big to be a puma. Could a tiger or lion gotten loose from that circus that passed through a few weeks ago?"

"Could be, Gordy," mused the first man as he checked his rifle and jacked a round into the chamber. He set the safety then began to study the tracks in greater detail. His companion did the same. "If it did, it's a hell of a big one by the size of those tracks."

1

"Sam, the woman's tracks just disappeared. That cat must have carried her off."

"Then why isn't there any blood, Gordy? No boy, this makes no sense at all. Agent Sawchuk, I hate to be the one to tell you this, but it looks like your tracker has been killed by some sort of giant cat. You and your partner better stay close behind us; that cat could be anywhere."

"The tracks suggest the cat is tracking our killer, Deputy. We should follow along."

"You don't seem too upset by the death of your tracker."

"She's not dead; she's with the tiger."

"What???"

"She's with the tiger, probably catching a ride, tracking the killer. She'll find him, and probably deal with him if he puts up a fight. I'll ask you to stand down your weapons."

"What? With a tiger on the loose? Stand down my weapon? There's no way in hell..." he got no further as he felt the cold metal of a gun by his ear. The woman was pointing her pistol right at his head.

"As the agent in charge, I command you to stand down your weapons," repeated Agent Sawchuk.

"As a woman with PMS and a gun at your head, I suggest you do as he says." The hard look in her eye left no room for argument. They lowered the rifles.

"Just what the hell is going on here, Agent?" Grudgingly, the deputy passed over his rifle as he spoke.

"I'll tell you," replied Agent Sawchuk, as he removed the magazine from the rifle, turned the weapon on its side and ejected the cartridge from the barrel. The round arced high into the air and he caught it deftly. A flick of the wrist popped it back into the magazine which he then clipped back into the rifle. Slipping the safety back on, he passed the rifle back to its owner. "We don't want you boys shooting anything you shouldn't. Now, keep the safeties on and don't shoot unless I tell you to."

"If either of you two even thinks about shooting my tiger, I'll blow your brains all over this mountain." Kylie spun her side arm back into its holster then retrieved the backpack.

"Your tiger?"

"My tiger. She and Ella are tracking the killer right now. They'll find him, probably kill him, and your town will be safe once again."

With a look of disbelief and fear, one of the deputies looked at the sky then spoke. "We should be heading back; there's a storm about to break and I don't want to get caught out here in a blizzard; especially not if there is a crazy woman with a tiger and a killer running loose. We can pick up the trail after the storm passes."

"Sorry boys, but we go on," sighed Agent Sawchuk.

"Then we'd better get a move on," growled the deputy as he slung his rifle over his shoulder and set out on the tracks of the tiger.

Kylie took up the rear again and continued to plod along. She was tired, too tired. They had been on the trail of this killer for weeks. She'd eventually tracked him to this small town, but then Ella had taken over as tracker. Deep woods stuff was definitely not Kylie's forte.

This hunt had started with the queen's nightmares. For several days she'd awakened, screaming, from dreams of gigantic wolves hunting and killing children. At the first sign of a murder the team had grabbed the case and set out. Kylie had no idea where the trail would end, but she hoped it would end soon. She was tired and cranky, and so was Ella. A cranky shape-shifting vampire is no fun to live with.

Kylie's reverie was broken by the battle roar of a sabre-toothed tiger. "Kylie, you take lead," barked Agent Sawchuk. as he stepped back to let her pass. "Remember boys, I'm right behind you. Don't shoot until I tell you to."

The tiger roared again, but its voice was mixed with barking growls of another animal. "So you let the woman go first?" sneered the deputy.

"It's her tiger," replied Agent Sawchuk, a grin playing at the corners of his mouth. "It'll kill anyone else who gets near unless Kylie's there. You follow her, and I'll follow you."

They caught up to Kylie a few moments later. She was standing at the edge of a clearing. In the small open space, a battle raged. The sabre-toothed tiger was there, but so was something else. It was a huge wolf, yet with almost manlike features. It was horribly fast and savage, but it was no match for the sabre-tooth.

The big cat had the wolf creature trapped against a cliff face. With nowhere to run, the beast turned at bay. As lithe and fast as the wolf-man was, the cat was equally as fast, and far stronger. The cat was a mountain of rippling muscle, especially in the front quarters. A swat from one great paw sent the creature crashing back against the rock face. It leaped back to its feet, searching madly for an avenue of escape.

There was none. There was only the curving face of stone soaring above, or the long fall to the frozen lake far below. The forest path was blocked by the tiger. In desperation it attacked the cat.

The battle was fast and furious. Both were bloodied when it was over, but the wolf man was down with the cat roaring above him. Knowing his end was near; the creature's features shifted slightly. He looked almost human, pleading as he reached toward the cat.

"Touranga engure astan oristle agnon." The words came with difficulty from those misshapen jaws, but the pleading in its eyes was easy to read. The big cat tilted her head sideways for a moment and the beast repeated the phrase. She backed away slowly and he staggered to his feet. With a nod of thanks to her he turned and leaped out into space, making no sound as he plummeted to the frozen lake far below. The ice shattered on impact and the broken body of the wolf-man sank into the icy waters. The body of a naked man would be found in the lake months later.

The tiger looked over the cliff for a moment then she turned back. The people at the edge of the clearing were all in shock, but the tall girl stepped forward. "Come to me, my darling girl," she spoke softly. Eyeing the others closely, the big cat came to the dark skinned woman, growling deep in her throat. Everyone stood very still as that mass of rippling fury slowly came to the woman and rubbed against her side.

"Here, my beloved beauty, here's Ella's backpack. Can you take it to her please?" Kylie rubbed the cat affectionately on the neck then the huge animal turned back to the forest, the backpack in its jaws. She stopped once to snarl at the two deputies then vanished into the trees.

"What the hell just happened here?" asked one of the deputies as they shook off the spell of fear cast by the presence of the tiger.

"We found the killer and he fell to his death," replied Agent Sawchuk.

"That the official version?" asked the second deputy.

"That's what will go in my report," replied the agent. "Do you want to write up how a sabre-toothed tiger fought a wolf-man and chased him off a cliff?"

"The official line sounds good to me, right, Gordy?"

"Oh yeah, we say anything else and we'll get locked up somewhere. What the hell was that thing anyway?"

"The military and secret government labs have been experimenting with genetic manipulation for years," sighed the special agent. "Things haven't always gone right, and sometimes things slip through their fingers."

"So, you guys are the clean-up crew?"

"Ah-huh, you could say that."

"But if we do, you'll have to shoot us," sighed the other deputy. "Okay, we've got it. Is that where you got the tiger, miss?"

Kylie smiled at the new note of respect in the man's voice. The colour of her skin didn't seem so important now. "Yes indeed," she grinned, "raised her from a cub. She'll find Ella, drop off the backpack then return to the van."

"So, where is your tracker?"

"I've been checking for signs of others like that lurking about." That rich contralto voice belonged to another tall woman. Both deputies straightened up a bit as Ella stepped into view. She was carrying an empty backpack. "He was alone. We need to hurry before the storm hits. There is nothing more for us to do here."

Both men had questions on their lips, but the three government agents set out, so the deputies followed close behind. It was a long hike back to the vehicles, but it was all downhill.

Somewhere along the way the deputies found themselves at the front of the line. The winds were picking up and the snow starting to fall by the time they reached the wrecked car of their fleeing killer. Their own vehicles were parked close by.

"Say, tracker, wasn't that backpack full when you joined us in the clearing up on the ridge?" The deputy was gazing quizzically at the pack Ella had just tossed into the back of the big four-wheel drive they had rented.

"No, whatever made you think that?" Ella climbed into the seat beside the pack with her back turned so he wouldn't see her smile.

"I could have sworn that dang thing was full," he muttered as he climbed into the truck with his partner.

"What was full?" asked Gordy as he gunned the engine and set out along the road.

"Her backpack."

"You think she stopped to dispose of something?"

"Yeah, and it was probably evidence."

"Who cares, Sam, the feds have the case, the evidence, and we're rid of a killer. It all works for me. All I want now is a hot meal and a cold beer."

"Ah, you're right, Gordy. There's no point wasting energy on it; they'll never really tell us anything anyway. Let's get home before this weather gets any worse."

Agent Sawchuk drove a bit slower than the two local men. The snow was falling faster and he was in an unfamiliar vehicle. As he focused on the road ahead, Kylie turned to Ella who was in the back seat. She reached for her lover's hand and squeezed it gently. "Ella, honey, are you all right?"

"Eh? Oh, yes, my darling Kylie, I am fine. I wasn't wounded all that badly and the damage has healed all ready."

"That's not what concerns me, sweetheart. You're being awfully quiet."

"Sorry, I'm just a bit disturbed by what happened up on that mountain."

"Ella, can you tell us what that thing was up there?" asked Agent Sawchuk, still tightly focused on the road ahead.

"I'm not certain, Terry, nor do I know what it said to me. I do know it was pleading with me for something, but it wasn't asking for mercy, at least not for itself. I only wish I could remember that phrase."

"Not to worry, my kitten, I have the whole show recorded on my phone."

"Kylie, you're a genius. Terry, we have to report to the king before you officially report in."

"I agree, but first I have to get us back to the hotel in one piece. This storm is really picking up." They continued on in silence for some time before the four-wheel drive forced its way into the hotel parking lot.

They fought their way through the storm and into the hotel lobby, shaking snow from their clothes and stomping their feet to clear their boots. They got a look of disapproval, yet nothing was said, as they picked up the room keys and headed for the elevators.

The girls were barely inside the room with the backpack on the spare bed when a light knock came at the door. Kylie opened it and let Agent Sawchuk in. He sank into a chair and passed a full wine bottle to Ella who eyed it suspiciously. "Wine, Terry? What's this for?"

"It's not wine, Ella, it's blood. I brought it along just in case of emergency. You've been in a battle and you haven't fed for days. This should tide you over until we get back to New York."

"Terry..."

"Ella, you can't go hunting in that," he sighed, gesturing at the storm outside.

"Agreed," she said, as she relaxed into her chair. "Where did you get this?"

"Miss Gudrun gave it to me before she left for Africa last week. She said I might need it if we were heading into the Oregon mountains this time of year. She didn't want me to get stuck in a storm with a hungry vampire."

"She's a wise woman, Terry," chuckled Ella, "and she likes you." He just blushed as she took a long swig from the bottle.

Kylie was grinning as she ordered room service for herself and Agent Sawchuk.

TWO DAYS LATER THEY were back in New York. They were picked up at the airport and driven directly into a rougher area of the sprawling city, to an office building with a warehouse attached at the back. Inside they passed the reception desk and went straight to the inner offices. A woman with a care worn face greeted them. "Everyone is waiting in the board room."

"Thanks you, Amanda, please join us," replied Ella, as she headed down the carpeted hallway. The others followed close behind.

"Greetings, my king." Ella smiled as she stepped through the door.

"Please be seated, people," replied the regal looking blond man with the wide shoulders. "Your message was a bit cryptic, Mother. Did you succeed?"

"We did, Harald, but I'm deeply concerned. The killer wasn't human, but neither was he one of our kind, as we had feared. Instead he was something I've not encountered before, but I believe Peter may have."

"Me? What do you mean, Mother?" The speaker was a short, heavy set fellow with a deep basso voice. That voice had a distinctly Russian accent.

"Ella. Please people, call me Ella. Yes, Peter. You once told me of a small tribe of people you encountered deep in the mountains of southern Russia. You said they were shapeshifters."

King Harald put his elbows on the table and leaned forward. "Shapeshifters? What kind of shapeshifters are we talking about? What did you find, Ella?"

"Perhaps it's better if we show you," said Kylie. "Tommy, can you put this video from my phone up onto the big screen?"

"Not a problem." The shy young man smiled as he accepted the phone from her hand and set to work. A moment later the huge screen leaped to life, and although the clip was a bit grainy, it was clear enough to follow. They all watched in silence until it was over.

As the screen went blank, Peter sighed deeply and leaned back in his chair. "Owan. I've not seen him for years. He was still a cub back then. Are you certain he's dead?"

"Can he revive as we do?"

"No, he cannot."

"Then he's dead, Peter," Ella replied kindly. "It was a long fall and he hit the ice then slipped beneath it. He didn't resurface."

"Someone must take word to his father. I guess that task falls to me."

"How do you know these people, Peter?" asked the king.

"Long ago, Sire, I was stalking a deer high in the mountains. I did not know a wolf pack was hunting too. We all charged at once. I had never seen another shapeshifter who wasn't one of us, and they hadn't seen any other except themselves. While we were looking each other over, the deer got up and ran away." Peter smiled and chuckled softly at the memory.

"Their leader stepped back and changed into a man, so I did also. They led me back to their camp and I spent several days learning to speak their language. It's very old and no other alive knows it, except their small band. They can also speak a dialect of Russian.

"Eventually we became friends, and I would visit them every few years or so. They're a shy people, preferring to stay hidden well back in their beloved mountains, never coming close to civilization.

"These aren't a savage people, Harald. I cannot imagine why he was here in America or why he so viciously killed those two young girls."

"Peter, what did he say to me?"

"He recognized who you are, Ella. I had told them many tales of the great cat who made me what I am. He said, 'Great Mother, protect my family.'"

Taking up the Quest

The room was silent for a moment as they absorbed that piece of information. Ella looked troubled and so did everyone else. Finally the queen spoke to break the silence. "Ella, did you bring me anything that belonged to this creature?"

"Yes, my queen." Ella passed over the small leather pouch that had fallen from the man's neck when he transformed into the wolf.

Accepting the pouch from Ella, the queen closed her eyes and began a series of deep breaths. Everyone remained silent. Sally had changed; rather she had blossomed, in the year of marriage to the vampire king. Harald doted on her and eventually she had adjusted to the new deference showed her by everyone, human and vampire.

She had become more self-assured, and took a great deal more pride in her appearance. Sally was indeed a beautiful woman and Harald beamed every time he looked at her. She had also opened herself to her psychic gift and was far more adept now.

Sally looked to be in pain as the vision took her. Expressions of fear, loathing, and horror crossed her face. Harald reached toward her, but Amanda put a gentle hand on his arm. "No, my lord, she has control now. Let her take command of it." He nodded and sat back as a snarl of pure hate crossed her countenance. Finally, with one last snarl, she sighed and opened her eyes. Tears began to run freely down her face.

The king reached for her hand. "What did you see, my love."

"Harald, we have to put a stop to this."

"Yes, my darling, and we shall. What are we putting a stop to?"

"They're torturing puppies, wolf-human hybrid puppies; teaching them to kill savagely."

"Who's torturing them, Sal?" asked Kylie.

11

"I don't know, Kylie, I couldn't understand the language. I think it was Russian, but I'm not sure."

"All right, my love, at least we're beginning to get a picture of what's going on. However, we need more information. Gudrun, did you hear of anything like this on your recent travels?"

"No, nothing like this, but I can check into it."

"Please do," replied the king. "Do we have any other information on this case?"

"Sire."

"Yes, Tommy?"

"Sir, I've got a news feed here. There have been two more killings in the past two days; one in Vancouver, Canada, and one in Washington DC. Sir, they're too far apart in space and too close in time to be the same killer." He passed a tablet to the king who glanced at the screen.

"Yes, and both seem to have occurred after the demise of Peter's friend, Owan. Add Sally's vision to that and we're starting to get a clearer picture. This thing seems to be organized; they're training captured children to be assassins. From what that one, Owan, said to Ella, we can assume they have blackmailed some of the adults into killing to save their cubs. People, I say we move on this immediately. Dissensions?" There were none.

"Peter, you take Gudrun with you and return to the homeland of these people. See what you can learn there, and let them know we will do all we can to help them. Agent Sawchuk, I assume your team will be assigned the case here in America. You will need Ella with you."

"Forgive me, Sire, but there could be a problem here."

"Explain."

"I'm expecting to be relieved of duty any day now. I've pushed the line pretty hard in the last year, and I get the impression I'm about to be replaced as team leader. Hell, I'll be lucky if they don't toss me in a hole somewhere and throw away the key."

"Are you serious?"

"Yes, sadly, I am. If they replace me, I'll be reassigned, but they'll want a full debriefing. They won't get it, not from me. I'll be accused of treason, locked away somewhere, and probably tortured for information. Paranoia runs pretty deep at the higher levels."

"Compton can't do that." Kylie leaped to her feet and began pacing about. "I'll quit too."

"As will I," said Amanda. The other members of the secret team all agreed.

"It seems we may have a problem," sighed Harald. "Suggestions?"

"You know what must be done, Harald." Gudrun had spoken softly, but all the vampires suddenly went quiet.

"He must be fully aware and make the choice freely, Gudrun."

"Fully aware of what, and make what choice freely?" asked Agent Sawchuk.

Ella reached over to grip his arm lightly. "Terry, there's a way to mark you so a vampire will always know where you are, and how you're feeling. It's something normally done between lovers.

"If you accept this you will develop strong feelings for the vampire who marks you. You will also constantly be aware of the vampire's emotional state. This is not something to take on lightly, for there is no way to reverse it."

"Have you marked Kylie?"

"Yes, and I'm sure the king has marked his queen, but we're lovers, Terry. The mark simply enhances the bond between us. This bond could create a very hard life for you if your feelings aren't returned."

"Better free and unloved than a prisoner locked away and tortured; I'm willing to take my chances. Does this mean you'll dig me out if they lock me away?"

"Terry, you're invaluable to us." King Harald smiled as he leaned his elbows on the table again. "As you can see, your team won't accept another leader. Just as I am leader of my people, so are you leader of yours. We need your people, and they need you."

"You could just make me forget everything."

"Agent Sawchuk," said Amanda, "you're not listening. We all made a bargain after the death of Mobutu last year. We swore to protect the vampires and they swore to protect us. We're irrevocably bound together with them, by our own choice.

"We agreed to help them survive in this world, and they agreed to help us protect the people of this country. We will all honour our vow to protect the people, whether or not we're sanctioned by our government. You know this, and you know we need you to lead us."

"You're right, Amanda, that oath will bind me regardless of who I work for. However, without the clout of the badges and the budget, it'll be a lot harder."

King Harald grinned as he spoke. "Agent Sawchuk, we can easily match your former budget as well as give you all an increase in salary. We can also equip your team with all they may need. As you say, it will be harder without your government connections, but we'll adapt. Besides, you haven't been fired yet."

"No, I guess I haven't," chuckled the agent. "Okay, so let's get back to this marking thing. Once it's done I fall in love with the vampire who marks me and will always know where they are and how they're feeling, is that right?"

"That's correct, Terry." Ella smiled kindly as she squeezed his arm once again. "It will be a lifetime of emotional anguish. Think it over before you decide anything."

"There's no time," declared Gudrun, rising to pace about the room. "We must act swiftly. We need Terry and his team. Surely you all understand the danger this situation puts us all in."

"Okay, so quit stalling and do it, Blondie." Gudrun spun and leaped to go nose to nose with the agent.

"Are you certain?"

"Just do it already."

"Come to me, Terry," she purred seductively.

She let her eyelids flutter closed as she slowly lowered her lips to brush his softly then pass along his strong jaw on the way to his throat. Suddenly sharp fangs bit deeply into his neck and he gasped. His body automatically tried to fight her, but he forced himself to remain still. Gudrun drank deeply of his lifeblood for only a moment then withdrew. Gently, lovingly, she licked the wounds until they sealed over.

"You are mine now, Terry Sawchuk. Now and forever."

"Then nothing has really changed, has it?" he replied as he sank into a chair.

"Terry..."

"I know, Blondie, I know. It's okay."

Just then the agent's cell phone rang. The king nodded and everyone fell silent. Flipping open the phone, Terry put it on speaker. "Sawchuk," he said, his voice somewhat shaky.

"Sawchuk, where the hell is your report? Are you in New York yet?"

"Yes, Director Compton, I'm back in the city. You'll have the report on your desk first thing in the morning."

"Tomorrow morning my ass, get in here right now and deliver that report. We need to debrief you and your whole team. What the hell are you thinking? Sawchuk?"

"I'm sorry, but I can't get there right now. I'll report in tomorrow morning."

"You sound sick, or drunk. What the hell is going on here, Agent?"

"I just gave blood, Sir. I'm pretty shaky right now and I need to rest. I'll report in tomorrow."

"Fine." At that snarl the connection was broken. Agent Sawchuk grinned and put away his phone.

"You just gave blood?" asked Kylie with an arched eyebrow.

"Did I lie?" He grinned. There was a round of chuckles at that.

"By the sounds of Compton's voice, I'd say we need to be prepared." The speaker was a small man with twinkling eyes.

"Clyde's right, we need a plan," said Amanda. "If we all go in and resign they'll want to debrief us all, and they have some very sophisticated equipment to help them."

"So do we," replied Kylie, "right Clyde?"

"Agreed, Kylie."

"Would you two mind sharing with the rest of us," grumbled the king.

"Sire, we need to be prepared," said Clyde. "What we need is to be able to give all the right answers to their questions, and we have to believe it ourselves. That's the only way to beat the machines. I suggest you put a compulsion on us that will make us forget any of you ever existed. Give us other reasonable stories to tell and make sure we all believe it."

"Give us the compulsion, but attach it to a command word," said Amanda. "One word to make us forget and then another to make us remember after all is said and done. If we don't need to resign, then the command need not be issued, but if we do..."

"I understand," said Harald as he rose to his feet. "Ella, your compulsion is the strongest of us all. I ask you to deal with this. We'll all reconvene here at sundown tomorrow to make further plans. Get some rest people." Taking his queen by the arm, he strode through the door.

As the royal couple exited the boardroom, Ella called the humans together...

NINE O'CLOCK SHARP, a thin man marched into the government building and headed for his office. He didn't look happy. As he reached his door, his secretary was at her desk and two men were waiting for him. "Good morning, Senator, Agent Sawchuk. Right this way." He led them into his office then shut the door before taking his place behind the desk. "Please be seated, Senator." He didn't asked Agent Sawchuk to sit.

"Let's cut to the chase, shall we?" he muttered as he shuffled some papers on his desk. He raised his eyes and glared at Agent Sawchuk. "Perhaps you can help the senator and I to understand some of your recent reports, Agent. For example, in the last year you've spent over three quarters of a million dollars on office supplies. Can you explain that?"

"As I understood my mandate, director, I was to guide my team in the location and control of unusual threats to the U.S."

"So?"

"Do you remember September eleventh, sir?"

"You know damn well I remember 9/11, agent. I barely got out of building one alive. What has that to do with your office supplies?"

"Did it happen again in Washington last month? Did it happen again in L.A. six months ago?"

"Of course it didn't, what the hell does that have to do with my question?"

"It didn't happen because we had the right office supplies, director."

"Really? So what about that team of European Mercs that have been working in the U.S. lately, you never did file a report about them. Why not?"

"Because they're the office supplies, sir."

"What??? Do you mean to say you've been using foreign nationals on American soil?"

"No, sir."

"Explain that, agent," said the senator, a hint of a threat in his voice as he leaned forward in his chair.

"Sir, in the past, too many of our problems have arisen because foreign nationals take refuge inside their embassies," replied Agent Sawchuk. "They plot murder and mayhem, and then run behind the magic doors and we can't touch them. I send them office supplies. End of problem."

"So you admit to wilfully breaking the law and your oath to uphold the laws of this great nation."

"I took an oath to protect the American people, and I've done just that."

"I want your badge, Agent. You're finished and your team will be assigned a new lead agent. That favourite consultant of yours will have to be dealt with as well."

"Ella West? You don't want to mess with Ella. If you remove me she will no longer work for the team anyway."

"Your badge and gun; on the desk now." Without another word, Agent Sawchuk laid his badge and gun on the director's desk. "Remember your oath, Agent, or should I say, Mr. Sawchuk. Your desk has been locked as has your computer. You will now hand over any and all files as well as the contact numbers for this Ella West and your "office supplies.""

Agent Sawchuk calmly reached into his pocket and pulled out his cell phone. He thumbed it open then hit the speed dial. It was answered on the first ring. "The goalie is down," he said. He then tossed the phone onto the floor where it burst into flame and melted into a useless puddle. "Clara Bynes, you're a bloody genius," he thought as he watched the shocked faces of the director and the senator.

"Sawchuk, what the fuck did you just do?" shouted the director as he triggered an alarm.

"I sent for some office supplies for you, director."

"Arrest that man," commanded the director as two guards burst through the door. Agent Sawchuk made no resistance as his hands were cuffed behind his back and he was led away.

Just outside the director's door they met a tall blonde woman coming the other way. She didn't look happy. *"You two, bring that man and follow me,"* she commanded. The vampire's compulsion cannot be broken or refused. They followed her back into the director's office.

"What the hell is going..."

"Be silent. You two, remove Agent Sawchuk's handcuffs." The two guards did as they were commanded. *"Now, you were never called to this office, you did not arrest anyone. Return to your posts and resume your duties."* They saluted and left the office.

"All right, Terry, how do you want to do this? Do you want your job back?"

"No, Miss Gudrun, I have a better idea. I think it'll work better if I'm a private investigator who works closely with the new team they put in place. They should disband my old team."

"Good idea, Terry, I like it." She turned those eyes of ice on the two men left in the room. *"Who commands here?"*

"I do," the director said in a shaky voice.

"You are to disband Agent Sawchuk's team immediately. He is now a private investigator with whom your new team, once formed, will work closely as he requires. There will be no need to debrief the former team members. Do you understand your instructions?"

"I understand."

"Then be about the business. You there," she said as she turned to the senator who was sitting quietly. *"Go out into the outer office and sit down. You will not remember anything that has happened inside this office today."* Without a word the senator stood and left the room. Gudrun took Terry's arm and followed him out.

The secretary was sitting quietly at her desk as Gudrun had instructed. Gudrun snapped her fingers and the girl came back to life. "Yes ma'am, can I help you?"

"No dear, that's all right," Gudrun responded in a thick New York accent, "I just came to meet my boyfriend. Come on, Terry honey, we're gonna be late." As they walked away they heard the secretary say that the director would see the senator immediately.

They entered the parking lot to find the entire team gathered around Kylie. "Hey, there's Agent Sawchuk," said Kylie. "Terry, what's going on, we just got fired."

"Yeah, I know, Kylie."

"So, who's the new girlfriend?"

Gudrun smiled and spoke a single word. "Vampire." There were puzzled looks for a moment then full memory flooded back as they began shaking off the spell.

"Wow, that freaks me out every time," said Tommy.

"It was necessary," smiled Gudrun. "Now, everybody back in your cars and return to the court. Harald will be waiting."

"SO, NOW YOU'RE A PRIVATE detective, Agent Sawchuk?"

"Yes, Sire, but I'm just Terry now. Agent Sawchuk's gone. I'll still have access to a lot of information, but that's about it."

"Actually, this may work out a bit better, Terry," said Harald. "You and your team now work for us. We'll set up offices for you all in this building and give you access to funds so you can carry out your tasks. Now, speaking of tasks, Peter, you and Gudrun get to Russia and see what you can learn there. Gudrun, can your people in Europe learn anything without triggering the wrong kind of attention?"

"I'll put Eric on it as soon as we arrive in Europe, Sire."

"Ella, take Terry and his team to Vancouver and see what you can do there. Gina, you hit the streets of the Italian district here in New York, see what you can learn. Jakob, Abel, Marlene, and Agnes are in France closing out some business. I'll contact them and see what they can find out there. Sally and I will go to Washington."

"Tommy and Clara should remain here with Gina," suggested Gudrun. "Their special talents are better used when they have access to all their toys."

"Good idea, Gudrun. What do you think, private detective?"

"She's right, Sire," chuckled Terry. "The team has to work differently now. Clara is better off in the lab and Tommy can co-ordinate the rest of us better from here."

"Then so be it; let's be about the business, people." The king rose and offered his hand to the queen. Everyone else stood and waited for them to leave before they all sprang into action.

On the Hunt

The rain was a soft, heavy mist that plastered the hair into his eyes. He didn't care; it just hid the tears that ran freely down his cheeks. Georg was completely tormented. He had stalked and killed an innocent young woman. Granted, her family, notably her father, was anything but innocent. That bit of rationalization didn't help, he had still murdered an innocent, his life would be forfeit and he knew it.

Shaking the mix of tears and rain from his eyes, Georg slunk deeper into the shadows. He was about to kill again. He had no choice. If he didn't complete his mission, all his children, his pups, would be tortured to death. Georg had no doubt this would happen for he'd been forced to watch as three young ones were thrown into the pits with half-starved fighting dogs. They'd had no chance, and their terrified screams haunted his dreams every night.

The approach of a car caught his attention, and he watched carefully as it slowed down then turned into the long driveway. The guards were lax, not expecting any trouble, and it had been relatively easy to slip past them and get over the fence. Filled with self-loathing, Georg caused his body to change. It would be easier for the wolf, but not much.

SALLY ELDREDSSON STRETCHED, then relaxed back into the arms of her lover, Harald Eldredsson, the Vampire King. "I know you're awake," she smiled, as she snuggled deeper into his embrace.

"How did you know?"

"I'm psychic, remember?"

22

"Yes dear, I do remember." He smiled as he lightly kissed her lips. "Did you sleep well?"

"Yes I did, lover. I must tell you how much I enjoy this sleeping all day. I always hated getting up early to open the shop. I much prefer to stay up half the night and sleep all day."

"So, you're nocturnal, too?"

"I'm getting there, my darling." She smiled as she kissed him deeply. "Was your hunt successful?"

"It was, my love. I won't need to feed again for many days."

"Well, I don't have that luxury, my fine Saxon king." She laughed as she sat up in the bed. "I'm hungry; I'm calling room service."

"You get some food, my darling; I'll check in with Tommy to see if anyone has learned anything. It's early days yet, but who knows." Harald reached for the phone, but Sally's gasp brought him up short. "Sally?"

"He's hunting, Harald," she replied, half in a trance, seeing a world he couldn't see. "My god, it's the baby he's going to kill." She shook off the trance and looked at her husband with pleading in her eyes. "Harald, he doesn't want to kill, but he must."

"Where?"

"I don't know. We need to get in the car and move around; I'll know when we're getting close."

"Dress swiftly, my love."

Within moments they were in the car and heading out. "I saw a long drive with gates and guards." Harald nodded and turned toward the more upscale areas of the city. A short while later she grabbed his arm tightly. "There, that place." He nodded again and drove by. A little farther on, he stopped.

"I feel like Batman with all this gear Clara has on me," he grumbled as he shifted into the half cat half man. He strapped on the belt with the weapons and tools that Clara Bynes had designed for him to carry in vampire form. "And I truly hate this spandex underwear."

"Hurry, my love, there's no time." With a half snarl the vampire easily leaped the high fence and disappeared into the grounds of the mansion.

Harold grinned as he noted the weapon's belt made no sound, nor did it hinder him in any way. He located the wolf and its target just as the wolf charged.

The young woman smiled and danced away from the car, swinging the laughing baby in her arms. Suddenly she screamed as a huge wolf sprang from the shadows and charged at her, great jaws reaching for the precious bundle in her arms. Just as the cruel fangs were about to close on the small body, something out of a nightmare or a bad movie appeared and tackled the wolf, knocking it aside.

The wolf turned at lightning speed, jaws reaching for the attacker, but the vampire was faster and stronger. The battle raged for a few moments, but the wolf was over matched, and he knew it. He fled with the vampire in pursuit. The woman was still screaming; her husband and his guards were shooting, but the creatures were too fast and they disappeared over the fence.

As the wolf leaped the fence and hit the ground running he felt a sharp sting in his side. He turned at full stride and saw a woman lowering a rifle. He felt the drug coursing through his system as she smiled at the vampire who approached. The wolf took another step toward her then his vision blurred completely, and he lost consciousness. As he fell to the ground his body changed back to the shape of a man.

GEORG AWAKENED SLOWLY. His head hurt and the rocking motion was making him sick. He groaned as he tried to open his eyes. "Better pull over, my love," rumbled a deep voice. "Our guest is waking up and he looks pretty green."

"There's a rest stop up ahead," replied a sweet musical voice. "I need to stretch my legs, anyway."

Georg felt the car slow then turn off the road. He managed to get both eyes to focus and recognized the woman driving as the one who had shot him. They stopped and got out of the car. His eyes roamed hungrily over the nearby forest, but her voice brought him back with a jolt.

"Don't even think about it, Wolfman. Try to run and Harald will make you sorry. Perhaps next time I won't use a tranquilizer dart."

"Georg, my name is Georg." He had a thick Russian accent, but they could understand him. "You would kill me?"

"You were going to kill that baby."

Tears filled the man's eyes as Harald threw a coat around his shoulders. "I had no choice."

"You always have a choice." Sally's voice was cold and unyielding.

"Yes, and I made the choice to save my own children. They are surely dead now, tortured to death. For this I will kill you if I can."

Sally rounded on him; her eyes ablaze with fury. Harald stepped between them, gently laying his huge hands on her shoulders. "This will not help, my love. Remember why we're here, what you asked me to do."

"I'm sorry, Harald." She sighed as she slumped against him. "You're right. Georg, forgive me, we're here to help you, not to harm you."

"Help me? You shoot me and cause my children to be killed; this is helping how?"

Her hand reached out to grasp his. Her eyes went out of focus for a moment then locked onto his. "Your children are still alive. Do you know where they are?"

"They're in Russia; there is no time. By now he will know I failed and will kill them."

"Do you have a way to contact this man?" asked Harald.

"I have a phone number, but what is the use? I have failed."

"Not yet you haven't," growled Harald, as he passed the man his cell phone. "Whoever he is, he wants that child dead, not your children. If he kills your children he no longer has a hold over you. Call him, stall for time."

Georg took the phone and began punching in numbers. He put it on speaker so they could hear. For some reason he wanted to trust these people. "Stephan, this is Georg."

"You failed. You know what happens now."

"There were too many guards, Stephan. I will stalk them; I will not fail. Do not harm my children, I beg you."

"One week, no more." The connection was broken.

"Well, that's bought us a little time," Harald said as he sat down at a picnic table. "Come Georg; sit for a few moments then we'll get back on the road."

Georg sat loosely, defeat clear in his posture. It took a moment for him to realize the woman was smiling at him. "Hi, I'm Sally." She offered her hand, and he took it hesitantly.

"Nice to meet you, Sally. Are you going to kill me?"

"No, Georg, we're going to help you get your children back."

"How can you do that?"

"We have our ways. Harald, my lover, the night's nearly gone. Do you want to find a motel for the day?"

"We should drive straight through, sad to say. We need to get Georg back to New York as quickly as possible." She agreed and volunteered to take another shift behind the wheel. "Gods, I hope it rains." Harald was still grumbling as they climbed back into the car.

Georg chuckled and followed. For some reason he felt safe with these crazy people. Perhaps there was hope. They were like Peter, and Peter had always been a friend. They were all quiet for a while then he spoke. "You are fast and strong, big man. You are like my friend Peter; a shapeshifter like us, except you are half tiger."

"That's correct," replied Harald. "Peter's a friend. He's gone to Russia to see what he can find out about all this. Tell me all you can of what happened to you."

Georg sighed and melted into the back seat, tears in his eyes. "It was about a year ago they came. Someone must have seen us and told of our existence in the mountains. They came with nets and tranquilizer guns. The young and several of our women were taken. One woman was sent back with a message to meet at a certain place.

"When we arrived they told us we must kill for them. We refused and they killed a woman to show they meant business. We transformed to attack them, but they had our young ones. There was nothing we could do. They want us to kill the children of their enemies."

"The children of their enemies?"

"That is what they told us, Sir. Can you truly help us; can you save our children?"

"We'll do all in our power to save them, Georg," said Sally.

"I hope it will be enough," he sighed, "or we will be the last of our people."

"RAINING," KYLIE MUTTERED, as they left the airport and found the rental van. "I'll bet Vancouver is just like Seattle."

"Relax girl, at least it isn't snowing," said Terry, grinning.

"Amen to that," chuckled Ella. "What's first on the list?"

"First to the hotel," replied Terry. "Then I'll make contact with the locals, Kylie, see what you can dig up, Ella, you go hunting so you're well nourished; Clyde and Amanda see what sort of profile you can come up with."

"Aye, aye, Captain Bly." Kylie laughed as she stowed their luggage in the back of the rental van.

A short while later they were set up in a suite of a nearby hotel, the Delta. Clyde was helping Kylie to set up the computer equipment while Amanda caught a nap. Terry dropped Ella off in what looked like a seedier part of town, then he sought out the police stations.

The police weren't too enthusiastic about having a foreign private eye poking around and Terry didn't learn much. After leaving the station he began to cruise the bars, asking around about a Russian guy, new to town.

Vancouver is a city with a lot of transients, so it didn't take long to get a few descriptions. He eventually narrowed it down to two who seem to have appeared shortly before the murder and then disappeared afterwards. He even had a name for one of them. He wasn't sure it would be any good, but it might give Kylie something to work with.

He arrived back at the hotel late. Everyone was asleep except Kylie. "Any luck?" she asked as he entered the room.

"Some." He sighed heavily as he sank into a chair. "I'll have to sharpen my skills a bit. I've become too dependent on that damn badge."

"I hear that; my access codes have all been cancelled. I had to hack in."

"Don't tell me that, Kylie."

"Why not? You're not law enforcement anymore."

"Good point. Well done, Kylie. Great job." He chuckled as he handed her his notebook. "There's three descriptions and a possible name. Have fun; I'm going for some shut eye."

"Sweet dreams."

"Thanks. Say, why are you still up?"

"I'm waiting for Ella; she'll be home soon."

"Did she have a successful hunt?"

"Doesn't she always?"

"Yeah, well, I guess a couple of million years of practice does give her an advantage. G'night, Kylie."

There was no response as she was focused on the computer screen. He smiled and closed the door behind him as he headed for his own room.

SOAKED FROM THE RAIN, a small Slavic looking woman stepped into the café and headed for a booth at the back. She removed her coat and shook off the water before hanging it on a peg. Her eyes remained downcast as the cadaverous looking man approached. "You want coffee?"

"Da, and some meat?"

He slouched away but soon returned with her coffee and some cold roast beef. "Who did you talk to, Olla? What did you say?"

She took a long sip of the hot drink then began to chew slowly on a piece of meat. "What do you mean? I have talked to no one. I have said nothing. Do you think I am so stupid?"

"Someone has talked out of turn. There was a man in here asking questions. He claimed to be an American private detective. He had your description, Olla, and your name."

"I spoke to no one."

"Stephan will not like this, Olla. Have you found your next target?"

"I have. Now I will begin to stalk them." She sighed and continued to study her hands on the warm mug. "Please don't tell Stephan of this. I'll be wary and I will complete my task."

"He will know anyway, Olla; he always does. Ah well, perhaps it does not matter. Magda has been reading the cards for you. She says you will soon face great danger, but you will have a change of fortunes. Your future looks bright, so she says."

"Let us hope she is correct. I will take up the hunt again tomorrow. In a few days I'll know their patterns and where I should strike."

"I will bring you more meat; you need to keep up your strength."

"Thank you."

She finished her meal then left the booth, heading back out into the rain. He had no idea where she went. He shivered and hoped Stephan never had reason to send an assassin after him. He wondered how she did it, for she carried no weapons he could see.

Olla slouched down the slick street then disappeared into an alley. She dodged behind an open dumpster out of the rain then stripped off her clothes. She willed her body to change, then a female wolf curled up on the pile of clothing and went to sleep. The clothes would be warm and dry for her in the morning.

Morning found Olla shivering as she swiftly shook the loose wolf hair out of her clothes then hastily pulled them on. "Why must I always shed so much?" She left the alley and walked several blocks downtown before stopping, first at a service station washroom to tidy up, and then at a sidewalk café for breakfast. She ate slowly, her eyes fastened on the office building across the street. Olla nodded slightly as several men followed one well-dressed man into the building. She rose and paid her check then hailed a taxi.

The cab dropped her off near a school in one of the better neighbourhoods in the west end of the city. Olla had to be careful here; homeless people were not common in this area. She didn't want to be rousted by the police. Olla watched patiently as the day passed, but it was fruitless. She saw the child, but there was no way she could reach him through the crowds of children and parents picking them up from school.

This would have to be done at the child's home. Olla wasn't happy about that; the house was gated and had keen-eyed guards. Ah well, it couldn't be helped. She found a bus stop and returned to the downtown area for a meal and to wait for darkness. As the bus rolled through the streets, Olla let her thoughts wander back to the day she had become an assassin.

It had been a sunny day, and the clan had gathered in a high meadow to relax and enjoy the first picnic of spring. The women had been busy spreading out the blankets and food, the men were gathering wood for a small fire to make tea, and the children were playing in the open space, practicing the shift from human to wolf and back again.

Olla had heard a strange noise, and then a helicopter suddenly appeared. Men with guns began shooting at them and they fled back into the forest. There was no safety there as the chopper dropped to the ground and the men pursued them into the trees. The women and children were urged on ahead while the men shifted to wolf and hung back to slow the gunmen down. Several were killed.

There was one narrow pass they had to get through to escape into the vast forests below. They rushed into the narrow pass to find it blocked. Suddenly great nets were hurled down on them. They shifted into wolf form, but it did no good, they were captured.

A tall man came toward them, holding a large gun in his hand. He came close and looked at them as they snarled and snapped, trying to reach him. "Change to human form," he demanded. They simply redoubled their efforts to reach him. He shot the wolf that got the closest. Horrified, they watched as she writhed in pain and shifted back to human form as she died. "Change to human form," he demanded again.

"What do you want?" asked Olla as she changed and struggled to stand upright under the weight of the nets.

"Tell them all to change or die." Olla made a gesture with her hand and slowly, one by one, they changed back to human form. "Which are your children?" At the sound of his voice Olla's children tried to hide behind her.

Suddenly several large wolves charged from the trees. The first three were cut down by gunfire and the rest fled back into the forest. Two of the wolves changed instantly as they died, the third changed as well. Badly wounded, Olla's mate tried to crawl to her. She screamed and tried to go to him, but the man with the gun struck her and forced her back. With pleading eyes, the dying man choked out a few words to Olla as life left him.

Stunned and deep in shock, Olla just stared blankly at the body of her dead mate. "What did he say?" asked the gunman.

He had to repeat the question twice before she tore her eyes away from the body and faced him. "He asked me to protect the family."

"Will you do as he asked?"

"I will." Olla turned fully to him and stood straighter, displaying her naked form to him. "Do with me what you want, just don't harm the children."

"Pah!" he spat on the ground at her feet. "I don't have sex with animals. I have a different use for you, all of you." He turned away from her and raised a loudspeaker to his lips. "You in the forest; come out or I will kill the women and children." He waited for a moment, but when nothing happened he turned and shot one of the women. "Do as I say or I'll kill them all."

Five men came from the trees. "Is that all of you?"

"We are all that survived," replied Owan.

"Good enough. Come forward."

They had been caged and taken by helicopter to trucks waiting on a road far down the mountain. The children and older women were taken in one truck and the rest in another. That had been that last time she had seen her children, and a full year had passed. In that year they had been trained in the language and ways of the western nations then sent to North America and presented with their tasks.

"Why must I kill these children?" Olla had asked.

"Their fathers are very bad men."

"Why not kill them?"

"You will, one day. They must be made to suffer first. Your children are well, Olla and beg to see you each day. You know the rules. Two kills saves one of your children. You have three children so you must make six kills before we let them go."

She had been forbidden to use a gun or other weapon; the kills had to be made in wolf form. Olla had pushed the revulsion at what she must do deep down inside. She also pushed her sorrow and loss down as well. Only after she had won freedom for herself and her children would she seek the deep woods and howl out her pain, only then would she allow herself to mourn.

Old Friends

Gudrun sighed as the plane touched down at the airport. Peter sat beside her, hands white knuckled and body tense as he watched the land rise up to greet them. She had to get him out of the airport and into a more open space before he collapsed. Poor Peter didn't like flying.

In a rental car and on the road at last, Gudrun passed a wine bottle to Peter. "Drink this; it'll make you feel better."

"Wine, Gudrun?"

"Blood, Peter. You look like death warmed over. Get some nourishment into you."

"Thank you."

"Still can't get used to flying?"

"If I was meant to fly Mother would have made me a bat instead of a were-cat." Gudrun chuckled and pulled out onto the highway. They still had a long way to go. Thank god he was relaxing at last.

It had been a long night on the road, but dawn found them camping at the base of the mountains. "I know this is a bit rough for a lady, but it's the best we can do right now."

"Oh please," sighed Gudrun, as she shifted into full vampire mode and set up the camp at super speed.

"Forgive me, Gudrun. You're so beautiful and poised; I often forget what it is you do for a living. This is probably quite tame for you."

"Nice recovery."

"Thank you." He chuckled as he settled back to look at the stars. "The sky is so very beautiful, isn't it?"

"Indeed it is, Peter, indeed it is."

"Gudrun, how are you feeling these days?"

"What do you mean?"

"Since we all moved to New York to be close together. Also, once more we're subject to a king as in days of old. How do you feel about all of this?"

"Hmm, well, on one hand I feel a bit constrained. I'm accustomed to choosing my own tasks and the order in which I do them. I also struggle with all the closeness at times. On the other hand, I feel more secure and less alone, if you know what I mean."

"I do indeed."

"I also trust Harald. I know he'll do a far better job of keeping us all alive than if we were on our own. It's also nice to know there's someone I can turn to if things get crazy. Having spent so many years as a mercenary, I'm well aware that the key to success and survival is instant and full obedience to command. Harald's in command now and I feel secure in that."

"As do I. I haven't felt this secure in centuries, and I'm willing to admit it. I am a bit surprised that Mother made Harald king, though."

Gudrun chuckled at that. "Ah Peter, Mother is such a wise woman. She wanted her lover back and knew Harald was the best bet to accomplish that aim. Mother also wants us all to survive, and we need to band together, have a structure, and a clear chain of command if we're to accomplish that. Harald was a good king once, and he will be now. Mother is too solitary to be the ruling queen. She knew that."

"I see the rightness of your analysis. Mother is a wise woman indeed. She knows she's the strongest, and you're the best tactician. Harald is the next strongest, a fine tactician in his own right, yet he is also a man with good political skills. He will need all of that to keep us from killing each other."

"I agree, but you know, Peter, Clyde and Amanda have been a great help there. I find I'm not nearly as bothered by the constant closeness as I once was."

"Ah, now that is a good thing to hear."

"Oh?"

"Yes, this way you won't be so tempted to eat me if I snore."

Her clear laughter floated across the land like the sweet ring of bells. "Get some rest, Peter."

It took a full day of hiking through the forest, climbing ever higher, to reach the scene of the shapeshifters' capture. The signs were old, worn away by weather and a hard winter, but Gudrun found enough. "There was a battle in this place, Peter. Here lies what's left of one of the bodies. There are spent shells here as well, on the rocks."

"That one was Sten," mused Peter, as he inspected the ravaged remains on the ground.

"How can you tell?"

"See this stone wrapped and fastened to a chain of human hair? Sten was Owan's brother. He wore this always, as his mate, Olla, had made it for him." Carefully, reverently, he removed the talisman from the rotting corpse. "I will keep this for her in case we manage to find them.

"Gudrun..."

"Yes, Peter, we will tarry here long enough to gather the bodies and bury them. They were your friends. The graves must be shallow, but we can pile loose stones on them."

"Thank you, Gudrun. I wasn't sure you would be willing to spare the time, but I do feel the need to do this for them."

"Spare the time to bury friends? Long ago, I laboured for weeks to bury a whole village, my village. If you think I wouldn't take the time, you don't know me as well as you think you do."

"No, I suppose I don't at that," he mused, as he knelt and gently lifted the bones of his friend. He carried them to a likely looking spot for burial then turned back to search for another. Gudrun laid another corpse beside the first. "You know, I believe none of us knows the others as well as we should. Do we? We've always been so solitary, rarely meeting, then quickly parting. Perhaps this new enforced closeness will help us understand each other better."

"I agree, my friend." Gudrun laid yet another corpse beside the others. They had gathered eleven in all. "Perhaps when this is over, and time permits, we should all make an effort to get to know each other better. Since our continued survival depends on our united efforts, we each should know the others' strengths, weaknesses..."

"Ever the soldier. That's not exactly what I meant."

"Oh?"

"I meant beyond that, Gudrun. I know nothing of your history, your likes and dislikes, etc. I truly would like to know more."

"Why Peter, I'm flattered."

He fairly howled with laughter. "See, I now know you're a coquette and a tease. You know full well I enjoy the company of men for pleasure and companionship. However, thank you for lifting my spirits.

"You're welcome." She laid another body down gently. "Alas, this seems to be all of them."

"Yes, these are all. Shall we begin to dig?"

He noticed she had shimmered into full vampire mode. "We can work faster this way. I will admit, I am anxious to continue the hunt for survivors."

"As am I." He, too, shimmered into the half cat/ half human vampire and began to dig a final resting place for his friends.

In the end, the day was too far gone for them to continue after the bodies had been laid to rest. As they stood gazing at the eleven fresh graves, Peter's voice rumbled out into the vast silence of the ancient forest. "Hunt well, my friends, and know this. I will avenge you if I can. Hunt well."

Gudrun patted his broad shoulder then spoke softly. "We'll rest here for a few hours until we get better light. I'll set up the camp over there where you can see them." With that she turned away and set to work, leaving him alone with his thoughts.

The next day they hiked for hours, deeper into the forests, ever climbing higher and higher. Finally, as night approached, they reach a ruined village. There was no immediate sign of life. "This place looks deserted, Peter."

"It is, but it's only a winter camp. Their homes are yet a day away."

"Then let's go."

They set out once again, this time continuing well into the night. Peter knew the way and felt a strange sense of urgency now that they were so close. They next day the found the main village.

"This was their home, one of them, for centuries, Gudrun. What could have happened to cause them to abandon their homes?"

"I don't know, Peter, but they don't appear to be here either. Where else should we look now?"

"You should look behind you, traitor." That voice was tinged with sadness, grief, and anger.

"I didn't betray you, Illya," sighed Peter, as he and Gudrun slowly turned around. There were about a dozen wolves converging on them with silent steps, their fangs bared. One old man stood before them. "We've come to learn what has happened to you and to bring sad news."

"Why should I believe you, Peter? You're the only one who knew of my people, where to find us."

"I didn't betray your secret, nor do I know what has happened here, Illya. I've come with news of Owan."

"What news of Owan?" asked a woman's voice as a wolf shimmered into a small dark haired woman. "What news do you bring of my son?" The other wolves began to change now, and Gudrun relaxed her fighting stance.

"Owan is dead, Anna," Peter said gently. "I am so sorry to bring this news to you." The woman fell to her knees as heart wrenching wails of sorrow were torn from her throat.

"He died with honour, Illya. It's because of Owan that we're here, that our king has agreed to help your people. He has sent us here to find out what happened and how we can be of help. Illya, we found traces of a battle. There were bodies there, and we buried them. Sten was among the dead."

"Yes, Sten is dead. This we knew. We are beyond help now, Peter," sighed the man as he slowly shrugged into a cloak that was brought to him by a younger man. Soon all had dressed themselves in their long cloaks of furs. "Our young people have been stolen, our pups taken, and our strongest males killed. We're all that is left of our people. Soon the children of the wolf will be no more."

"We'll get them back for you, old friend," replied Peter as he rested his hand on his friend's shoulder. "This woman is the greatest soldier alive. She and her people will help us."

"Please, Peter, how did my son die?" asked Anna. "I've had such terrible dreams of late. In the dreams I saw him fall."

Peter's shoulders sagged as he sank to the ground. The others sat as well and listened. "Owan was forced to do terrible things," he began in that deep resonating voice. "Owan stalked and killed two young women."

"No, Owan would not..."

"Sadly, he did, Anna. I have no doubt that he was forced to do this, but he did kill them. Our mother was the one who tracked him. High in the mountains, Owan turned at bay and faced the great cat."

"The old one; the true cat you have spoken of so many times, the Great Mother?"

"Yes, Owan faced the tigress and lost. He could never have hoped to defeat Ella, but he knew who he faced. At the end he begged her to protect his family then he leaped off the cliff to the ice below."

"Here," said Gudrun gently, as she passed them a small screen. The couple watched in silence as their only son battled the tigress and lost. They saw him speak, the tigress back away, and they saw him leap to his death below. "This man gave his life to find help for you. Do not refuse the help he paid so dearly to bring to you. Tell us what happened here."

They spoke then of the attack in the summer fields, of how their people were taken, and of the deaths. They knew no more than that.

"This man who commanded them, what did he look like?" asked Gudrun.

"He was tall, with gold hair like your own, and a scar down his right cheek. He had only three fingers on his left hand."

"Stephan Krebs." A snarl of disgust crossed Gudrun's face. "I might have guessed; this has his stench all over it."

"You know this man, Gudrun?"

"All too well, Peter. We must be careful, but we now know who we're dealing with, and I have a good idea where we might find him. We must return to Moscow as quickly as possible. We'll need Eric."

"Can you truly help us?" asked Anna, a faint glimmer of hope in her eyes as she gazed imploringly up at Gudrun.

"We can and we will," Gudrun replied gently, as she sat beside the distraught woman, "but you must help yourselves as well."

"How? What more can we do? We don't know who these men are, where to find them, or why they took our people, especially the children."

"I can imagine. Our queen wants us to stop what's happening to your children. Our king wants the whole thing stopped, your people freed and safe, and he wants all knowledge of you and your people removed from the awareness of the world. I agree with his reasoning.

"However, this is what I meant when I said to help yourselves. You've hidden in these mountains far too long. The world has changed, and you must change with it. My people can teach yours how to survive in this new world, but you must be willing to learn."

"What must we do, Golden Lady?" asked Illya.

"You may call me Gudrun, Illya, all of you. I'm a friend, like Peter. How many of your people are left free?"

Both Illya and Anna pulled away from her at that. "You can trust Gudrun, Illya," said Peter, laying his hand on the man's shoulder.

"Please, my friends, the future of your people is now in her hands. Trust her."

"There are perhaps twenty in the forest," sighed Anna. "Only two children, one woman of childbearing age, and our elders; why do you ask our numbers?"

"I need to know how big the plane should be," replied Gudrun, a twinkle in her eye.

"The plane?"

"I want to take you all to a safe place where our people can protect you and teach you the ways of the modern world. Once you have the proper skills, you can return to these mountains. With the right training no one will ever be able to sneak up on you again."

"Is such a thing possible?" Anna sighed and spoke again. "You are generous, Gudrun, but I fear there are too few of us left now. Our people will soon die off and be no more."

"Most of your people who were taken are still alive, Anna," replied Gudrun. "Our queen can see many things and she has seen that they're still alive. We'll set them free, but we must be careful. The man who took them is extremely dangerous. Fortunately, he's also quite secretive. He'll keep his captives away from prying eyes."

"You know him well, Gudrun?" asked Peter.

"Oh yes, he was once one of my men, but he couldn't be trusted. Stephan Krebs has one over-riding ambition; he wants to control all crime in the world. He thinks he is the only one intelligent enough to do this. He's also quite ruthless and without mercy."

"Are you planning to tell the king that you're bringing company home?" chuckled Peter.

"Of course," she replied. "If you would be so kind as to pass that SAT phone to me, I'll call him right now." Peter fished the phone from their small pack then passed it to her. He grinned as she dialed, hoping she would put it on speaker. She did.

"SAWCHUCK AGENCY, TOMMY speaking."

"Tommy, it's Gudrun. Is the king available?"

"I'll buzz you through, Miss Gudrun. One moment."

"Gudrun?"

"Harald, I have news."

"Sally says to bring them here so Tommy and Clara can teach them how to survive in the modern world." Peter roared with laughter at that.

"Tell her majesty that she's no fun at all," groused Gudrun. "Harald, I know who's done this and I think I know where we might locate him, but we must be careful."

"That's good news. Gudrun, we're on the clock here."

"I'll be swift, my king." She passed the phone back to Peter. "Illya, gather your people as quickly as you can. We must hurry." He nodded then threw his head back and gave a long mournful howl. It was answered from several directions.

ONCE THEY SET OUT THE return trip went swiftly. It was all downhill and the shapeshifters ran in wolf form. The vampires transformed as well. Thirty-six hours later, Peter and Gudrun stood by the side of a lonely road, watching as a Russian Air freighter slowly sank to the ground and taxied up to them. Illya and Anna waited with them. When the plane stopped Anna signalled and the other twenty-three of her people came out of the trees.

"Eric, did you have any trouble?" asked Gudrun, as she helped the villagers into the plane.

"None at all."

"You've been briefed?"

"Yes, by the king himself. Where are we going?"

"Helsinki."

"Gudrun, are we going after Stephan at last?"

"We are, but first I want to make sure he's where I want him to be." She turned to face Peter who was waiting by the car. "You know what to do?"

"I do, Gudrun; we'll be waiting."

She nodded then turned and leaped aboard the plane. "Go carefully, Eric. I don't want to be seen."

"Below the radar as usual," he grinned. Eric began to rev up the engines and Peter sped away in the car, his phone already at his ear.

Gudrun was nearly overwhelmed by the scent of fear in the enclosed space. It pulled at her hunting instincts, begging her to change, to kill, to feed. She fought it, but realized it would defeat her, she had to do something. Savagely pushing back the desire for blood, she rose to her feet and called for everyone attention.

"Listen to me, people. Hear me, listen carefully." Once certain she had their attention she put the compulsion on them. *"Listen carefully. You are enjoying this new experience. You're having fun, enjoying the adventure."* She sighed with relief as the fear subsided, and with it, her instinct to hunt, her punishing desire to kill. To feed. She would survive until it was time to jump and leave them with Eric. And so would they.

Capturing an Assassin

"How was the hunting?" inquired Kylie, not looking up from her computer screen.

"Quite good, actually," replied Ella, as she gracefully sank into a chair at the table, reaching over to gently stroke Kylie's cheek. "I'm well fed and now sleepy. Can you put that aside long enough for a cuddle with a vampire?"

"Sorry, lover." Kylie pushed the computer aside then rose to slide into Ella's lap. "You know how focused I can get."

"Yes, I know, that's why I'm trying to reset your focus onto something much more fun." Kylie sighed as Ella's lips gently traced the line of her jaw, then gasped slightly as she felt the fangs rub across her throat to be replaced with soft lips. "So, is it working?"

"Oh gods, yes." Kylie locked her lips on Ella's mouth, hungry for her, claiming her. With a purr of delight Ella rose easily with Kylie in her arms and carried her to the bed.

While Ella slept in Kylie's arms, Olla stalked her prey. She'd contacted Stephan and gained a few days grace, but this still wasn't going to be easy. She silently wept bitter tears and hid her face from passers by. How it tore at her soul to ravage these innocent children. Yes, their fathers might be evil, but why not kill them instead. This she would be able to do with an easier conscience.

As the grey foggy day slowly crawled towards darkness, Olla waited in the shadows of the alley and mourned. Mourned for her mate, the children she had killed, and for her own children she feared she might not be able to save. She did not believe Stephan would keep his word.

At last the man left his office to return home. That's where his children would be, and this is how Stephan wanted it. He wanted the man to watch as his children were torn apart. Olla swept her sorrow

44

aside and steeled herself for what she must do. She stepped towards the mouth of the alley to call a cab, but there was a tall woman blocking her path.

ELLA YAWNED AND STRETCHED like a contented cat, which she was. Alone in the bed, she swept her arm across the space beside her. It was still warm. Rolling over she saw Kylie, head down over her laptop computer. "Do you never sleep?"

"Daily, my beloved, and like a baby in your arms."

"What time is it?"

"The day is wearing on."

"Have we got anything?" With the grace that epitomized her, Ella rose to peer over Kylie's shoulder. "Street cameras? How did you..., never mind. Are we watching for anyone in particular?"

"Olla."

"Who is Olla?"

"Right now she's just a name and a hunch. Terry came up with the name of a Russian woman, homeless, sleeps in alleys, and yet is surprisingly strong as well as well fed. She also spends a lot of time in a bus stop near an office building owned by a local suspected crime boss. I think she's our target."

"I'll trust your instincts on this one Kylie. How did you learn all this?"

"Terry. He still smells like a cop to the street folk, but this girl Olla makes them nervous too. They were willing enough to talk for a few bucks and some coffee."

"Here's a picture of her that Terry got with that new camera Clara had rigged for him." Kylie clicked open a new screen.

The picture showed a poorly dressed woman of Slavic descent. Ella instantly recognized the look of a fellow predator. "Where's Terry now?"

"Out looking for her."

"Perhaps we should join him. Can you locate..."

Kylie's phone buzzed, it was Terry Sawchuk. "Kylie, I've got her in sight. I'm at the St. Vincent de Paul Thrift Store on East Hastings St. She's in an alley across the street."

"Okay, Terry, I've got you on camera. We're on our way. Don't lose her."

"That'll cost ya, Kylie." The phone went silent.

Grinning with mischief Kylie grabbed her coat and bag. Stuffing the laptop into the oversized bag, she headed for the door. "Come on, Ella. Hurry."

"Right behind you, oh impatient one." Kylie's eyes opened wide as Ella stepped into a pair of loose shoes and pulled on a long coat. She was naked beneath. "I have a feeling we may need the cat." She winked and licked her lips as she swept up her purse and followed Kylie.

Kylie groaned and sighed as she held the door open for Ella. "How the hell am I supposed to concentrate when I know you're buck naked under that flimsy coat?"

"Self discipline?"

"Right. Discipline. I can do it, sure I can." Ella was still chuckling as they reached the ground floor. They stepped outside where Kylie hailed a cab and gave the address.

"Ah, that's not the best neighbourhood, ladies," commented the driver as he pulled away from the hotel.

"We're detectives. We have an appointment with a source. Could you step on it a bit?"

"Okay, if you're sure that's where you want to be. Not my problem. Just as long as you're still alive..."

He continued to prattle on as he sped across the city. Ella ignored him as she gazed sadly out the window at the density of the concrete jungle. How she longed for the great forests this area was known for, but she wouldn't get to see them. They'd leave here and return to another concrete jungle.

Kylie patted Ella's knee. "Easy, lover. Easy. I know what's going through your mind and I agree, you do need a chance to run through the trees. It's been too long. Maybe when we get this done we can take a few weeks and visit the Yukon or some such place."

"I'd like that." Ella's smile broke the pensive mood just in time for their arrival. She paid the taxi fare while Kylie located Terry. He wasn't far away.

"It's my guess her target or target's parents work in that building down the street. She was watching it at lunchtime. Marking her prey's habits. Business is about done for the day so I expect she'll be on the move soon." There was a sudden blare of a horn as a car swerved to avoid Ella as she crossed the busy street.

"Dammit, Ella," muttered Terry as he started to follow her, but Kylie just caught his arm and shook her head. "All right, I'll warm up the car." Kylie nodded, never taking her eyes off Ella's retreating back until she disappeared into the alleyway.

Olla gazed at the tall woman for a long moment. Every instinct she had was screaming at her to run. For some reason she couldn't name she feared this woman. Perhaps she could bluff her way out. If not she might be able to frighten her away by changing into the wolf. It was her only chance. "Move aside and let me pass. I have no wish to harm you."

The tall woman just gazed at her for a long moment. When she spoke her voice was rich and full of command. "Are you Olla?"

"What if I am?"

"Are you planning to kill a child?"

Olla's hair began to rise on her neck and arms. She knew, but how could she know? "Move aside or I will make you move."

"Try."

That single word did more to shake Olla's confidence than a gun would have. She shrugged out of her dress and stepped out of her shoes, shimmering into the wolf. A snarl peeled back her lips as she took a single step towards the woman.

Ella dropped her coat and shimmered into the cat. Great fangs gleamed in the fading light as the massively muscled tiger stretched and advanced towards the wolf. A coughing growl passed her lips as she snarled in the face of the wolf. A clear challenge and a promise of death at the same time. The wolf shimmered back into a woman.

"I know who you are," Olla said, fear causing her voice to tremble. "You're the old one, the one tiger, the mother of Peter's people. I beg you kill me swiftly. I won't try to fight you." To her surprise the tiger shimmered back into the tall woman.

"Put your clothes on and come with me," said Ella, as she swept up her coat and purse. She stepped into her shoes and waited for Olla to join her. "My people wish to speak with you. There will be no more killing of children."

Olla burst into tears. "But I must or he'll kill my pups. I've seen him do this to others. The pups were torn apart by fighting dogs. Please."

Ella reached to pull the distraught woman into her arms. "Our people are already working to free your children, Olla. Come with me. Listen to what they have to say." A big car suddenly pulled up at the mouth of the alley and they climbed into the back seat.

Olla sat quietly, cuddled into the tall woman's arms. She had been on her own for too long and it felt good to be held and comforted, even if it was by the most dangerous person in the world.

The burly man behind the wheel drove out of the city then headed east. "Terry, aren't you going the wrong way?" asked the dark skinned woman who was smiling at him.

"Nope. I know of a place about an hour away. We go up into a high valley above a tourist spot. The Canadian and American borders touch there in a wooded area. Ella and Olla can transform and slip across the border easily while we backtrack a bit to a guarded crossing. We cross into Washington State, then swing around and pick them up."

"You're a devious man, Detective Sawchuk," grinned the dark girl as she winked at Ella. The driver turned off the highway at a sign that said Cultus Lake.

"Great Mother, what will become of my children?"

"I cannot say, Olla," replied Ella as she stroked the hair back from the woman's face. She shook her head sadly, this woman was barely more than a child herself. "We'll take you to our people. Our queen will be able to tell you more of your children and the king will need to know all you can tell him to help stop this madness."

"You are not the queen?"

"No, Olla, our queen is a human, but she is the queen. She's very wise, as is the king."

"I fear my pups are already dead, as is my mate. I believe Stephan probably has already killed my young, but I was afraid to disobey him, just in case."

"I understand. The queen will be able to tell us more. Meanwhile, your friend Peter and Gudrun are already searching for the children of the wolf."

"Who is Gudrun?"

"She is one of us," replied Ella. "She's the greatest soldier alive. If anyone can retrieve your children it will be Gudrun."

"Do you believe in her so strongly?"

"I do, for it was she who returned my love to me from a deadly and fearsome enemy." Olla smiled for the first time as she saw Ella reach for and gently squeeze the dark girl's hand.

"Here we are, ladies," said Terry as he stopped the car on a lonely stretch of road. "Across that field is American soil. I'll stop and let you out once we're out of sight of the houses."

The big car stopped and Olla reluctantly left Ella's arms. They got out and tossed their clothes in the trunk then shifted into wolf and tigress. The car sped away as the two beasts slipped into the forest. Ella let out a groan of contentment as she shook herself then trotted off towards the border. Olla followed close behind. Darkness had fallen and the moon was well up before the big car pulled up near the two beasts.

Soon Olla was back in the big car, this time cuddled into the arms of the dark girl. Late the next day she was in the presence of the king and queen of the vampires, telling them her story.

When she finished speaking, the queen held out her hands and Olla took them in hers. The eyes of the queen went out of focus for a moment then snapped back. "Your children are alive, Olla, all three. Harald, that man is getting nervous. Time is running short."

The king nodded then signalled for another to approach. "Any news, Tommy?"

"Sire, the rest of Olla's clan are on a plane bound for New York. Gudrun has made arrangements to get them into the country unobserved. I expect we'll have a houseful soon. Clyde and Amanda are setting up quarters for them right now. Miss Gudrun was dropped into Finland, but that's all I know."

"She's hunting, and she's not happy," said Terry. "I have no idea why, but I'm glad she's far away right now. She's superbly pissed."

"That means the quarry has slipped her grasp," sighed the king. Just then his phone rang. The room fell silent as he answered. "Gudrun, report." He popped it on speaker.

"I arrived a day too late, Sire. The one human remaining at this place said he moves the captives around, only remaining in one place for a couple of days. He didn't know where Stephan has gone, but I have a pretty good idea. I'm on the road now and should be in Sweden soon. I'll report in the instant I have news.

"Oh, and tell Terry to stop sulking. It's buggering up my concentration." With that she was gone. Terry just chuckled and shook his head.

"All right, people. Conclusions? Suggestions? Ideas?"

Ella stood and began to pace. Finally she stopped, facing the king. "Our prey may have clued in that he's being hunted, or not, Sire, but it matters little. Gudrun will find him. I suggest you and I remain ready for travel in case she should call for our assistance.

"In the meantime perhaps we should focus on our guests. They'll need to learn to survive in this modern world, and the transition won't be easy. There's also the matter of their health. They're a hardy folk, but Olla tells me they can be susceptible to some diseases. They'll need to be studied."

"Studied?" Olla was on her feet, the fear easy to read in her posture and her eyes. "You wish to dissect some of us as that man has done?"

"No, Olla, not ever," replied Sally. "That isn't what was meant. We wish only to learn what we can about you, how it is that you can have children and the vampires can't, but reproduce in another way. What would happen if one of you mated with a regular human. Would the child be human of wolfkind? If one of you mated with a vampire could there be children of that union? I swear to you no one will be harmed in the process."

"Wolf and vampire can't have children," Olla replied softly, visibly relaxing again. "It has been tried and failed, Peter can tell you. With humans, I have no idea. So, you want to know everything there is to know about us. Why?"

"We're curious," smiled the king. "Cats are ever curious, you know this."

Olla smiled in return. "So they are. Ah well, what will it hurt now. We've always been so careful to hide ourselves and everything about us. You've been so very good to me. Great Mother didn't kill me, but nurtured me, as did Kylie. All have been kind. When the clan arrives, I'll speak to them to allay their fears. Will this be helpful?"

"It will be most helpful, Olla. Ah, here comes Amanda. She will take you to a place where you can rest."

The stern looking woman led Olla to a room with a bed and a few bits of furniture. She also showed her the washroom, explained how the amenities worked, then left her to her own devices. Olla luxuriated under the warm shower for a long time then dried herself off and returned to the bedroom. There was a small table loaded with food waiting for her there.

Olla ate her fill then sighed with contentment, shifted into the wolf and curled up on the soft bed. Her belly full for the first time in weeks, and her mind somewhat at ease that her children were still alive. These people were trying to rescue them; she drifted off into a deep dreamless sleep. She awakened many hours later to a knock on the door and Amanda's voice.

"Olla, wake up. Your people are here, and they're terribly confused. Come quickly."

Olla shifted back into human form and dressed swiftly. "Still shedding," she muttered as she noticed the hair on the bedding. "Coming," she called as she reached for the doorknob.

Hunted

The two men watched the video of the blonde woman searching their hideout in Finland. Fortunately for them they were in Norway.

"Who is she, Stephan?" asked the heavily muscled man. "She moves like a warrior."

"What else do you see, Marco?"

"She's angry, but controlling that emotion. She's quite beautiful as well; I'd like to meet her one day."

"No you wouldn't," replied the taller man. "Her name is Ariel. At least it was the last time I saw her. Ariel Swensen is the most dangerous woman you could ever encounter. If by some mischance you ever do meet her, Marco, do not challenge her."

"Seriously? I mean, she moves like she has skills, but surely she's not that good."

"You've been warned," replied his companion as he turned away from the screen. "Ariel. We did not part on good terms. If she's seeking me now there can be only two possible reasons."

Marco turned away from the vision of beauty on the small screen and followed his employer. Stephan seemed worried, and Stephan Krebs never worried. If the woman could rattle his cage she had to be someone special. "And those are?"

"She either needs me for an especially difficult mission, or she has been sent to kill me. I shall assume the latter."

"Oh? Why?"

"We've caused our competitors in America a deal of personal grief. I expect one of them has commissioned Ariel to extract vengeance. Dammit!" He punched his fist through the wall in frustration. "Why

53

now? We have no time for this." Stephan sighed deeply and sank into a plush chair where he sat brooding.

Marco stood and gazed out the window at the rich Norwegian Forest outside. From the outside the place looked like a private resort or hunting lodge, but it was owned by Stephan and was in reality one of his favourite hideouts.

"Should I go back to Finland and take care of this for you?"

"Marco, have you heard nothing I've said? Ariel would chew you up and still be hungry. Besides that, by the time you arrived she'd be in Sweden. She's very methodical, is Ariel. She'll search every place we have to hide until she finds us."

"She knows that much about you, boss?"

"Much of it. In my younger days I worked for her as a mercenary. She certainly has a way about her. Yes, she knows, or will soon know. If she wants to find you, you'll be found. Still, she came alone. If it was a kill mission, she'd have brought a crew."

"A crew?"

"Mercenaries. Former soldiers. Some of the best in the world." Stephan leaned forward in his chair to rest his arms on the desk. "So why did you come alone, Ariel? This is the thing that disturbs me the most. If you wanted to talk to me there are other more conventional ways to get in touch. If you wanted to kill me you'd have brought your soldiers.

"No, there's something else going on here. I must solve this puzzle. Why now? Why alone? You've ignored me for years. You were angry when we parted, but always we were content to ignore each other. There was, and still is, no profit for either of us to go to war.

"So, what's different now? Is it my attack on the American crime syndicates? Are you involved with one of them? No, even if that were true, how could that have been connected to me? I've kept everything at arm's length. Those in America know which organization has attacked them, but not who runs it."

"Maybe it's the mutants," suggested Marco. "That's new."

Stephan rubbed his chin thoughtfully. "True, this is definitely different, but what possible connection could this have to Ariel? There are too many unanswered questions. Unanswered question make me nervous. What could possibly connect us there?"

"One of our assassins has disappeared in Canada and another in the States. Perhaps the lady has captured one of them."

"Yes, yes, that must be it, Marco. Good thinking. Yes, someone has spent a vast fortune to hire the finest bodyguards in the world. Yes. Ariel has taken one of the animals alive and tortured it for information."

"Would any of them talk? Would they dare? Even if they did, why would she believe their story?"

Stephan rose to his feet and began pacing about the plush office. "Any of them would talk to Ariel. I remember that everyone always talks to her, and still I have no idea how she does it. She'd take a man to a room alone, we'd hear no screams of pain, but we would hear his fear filled voice spilling his guts. Yes, they would talk to Ariel.

"So, this is more than a simple bodyguard task for her. We can assume she's caught and interrogated one of them then reported to her employer. Said employer must have sent her against us."

"So, what now?"

"Now, Marco, we must prepare for war. It'll take her some time, but she will locate us. We'll make that as hard for her as possible. Gather up everything and prepare for evacuate."

"Where are we going this time?"

"We'll go to Scotland. She can't know of that place, so it'll take some time for her to find us. That island is also far easier to defend than any of the others."

"What of the other assassins in America? Should we call them back? Do we warn them?"

"No, we cut them loose. Maybe some of them will succeed, maybe not. I really don't care at this point."

"What of the young ones? Do we kill them and travel light?"

"No, we keep them. We'll need them as assassins in the future. Perhaps we can even send a few of the older ones against Ariel. No, Marco, take them to Scotland. I'll join you there."

"Boss? Where are you going?"

"Denmark. That'll be Ariel's next destination. I intend to make contact with her and see what I can learn. Oh don't worry, Marco. I'll only speak with her by phone. I'm not fool enough to get close to her, but I do want to be close enough to see her reactions. That could tell us much."

"All right, Stephan, you do what you must. I'll get the operation to Scotland unseen."

Marco walked outside to begin the preparations for leaving. He had never seen Stephan Krebs so rattled. It worried him. Stephan was the closest thing to a friend he had ever known, but that made no difference at all. If Stephan was coming unglued he would have to seek other employment. If there was anything Marko was, it was a survivor. He'd do his job to the best of his ability, but it was time to start watching for other opportunities.

STEPHAN KREBS ALWAYS had mixed feelings when he returned to Denmark. It was the land of his birth and early years, but it was not home. He had no home, nor a real concept of what the word home should mean. He had grown up in Copenhagen, on the streets, he knew the city well, that was as close to a home as he would ever get.

As a boy, Stephan had learned that the biggest and strongest could stop the others from fighting. The biggest and strongest could enforce peace, even if it was through violence and intimidation. For reasons of his own, Stephan wanted peace, peace at hand and peace on a global scale. There was only one way to get it. If the criminals controlled everything, as his father had said, then he had to become the biggest and strongest criminal.

Peace, the elusive dream of so many, but none truly had the courage to create it or the strength to enforce it. The answer was so simple he wondered that no one had thought of it before. First he had to gain control of crime on a global scale. Once he had full control of all the criminals he could create world peace and enforce it. He would be the man in control, none would dare defy him.

Stephan sighed deeply as he pulled up in front of the hotel, his reverie over. Time to get to work on the task at hand. Once he had settled into the hotel he contacted a man he knew. "A tall blonde, Stephan? That describes most of the women in Copenhagen," laughed the voice on the phone.

"Yes, I suppose it does. Listen carefully, she may already be at the old hideout. If not she will soon arrive. Her name is Ariel. Stay well out of her reach. Just verify her name then give her the phone. I have already picked it up and left it in an envelope at the front desk for you. Deliver the phone then get away from her. Go to the defense station as quickly as you can. Set the remotes, then get as far away from there as possible."

"She sounds dangerous, Stephan."

"You have no idea." He sighed as he closed the connection. All he could do now was wait.

It was early the next morning he got the call. "The phone has been delivered, Stephan. The remote is set, and I'm well clear. Unless I hear from you I'll return this evening to dispose of the body."

"Excellent. Your payment will be at the front desk first thing tomorrow morning."

Stephan Krebs sat staring at the phone for several moments then he set it back on the cradle. Taking out a new phone from his pocket he dialed and waited.

"What do you want, Stephan?"

"Ariel, it is good to see you again."

"I no longer use that name. You may call me Gudrun. So, you're watching me on video. Do you like what you see?"

"As always, Ariel, pardon, Gudrun, you are the most beautiful of women. The years have been kind to you."

"What is it you want, Stephan?"

"Actually, Gudrun, the question should be, what is it you want? You've been tracking me ever since I left Russia. What is it you want?"

"A meeting, Stephan."

"For old times' sake, eh? Getting sentimental after all this time?"

"Hardly. I have a task for you and your people."

"Indeed? What sort of task might that be, Ariel, that you would not do yourself?"

"Meet with me and find out," she replied.

Stephan continued to drink in the sight of her. She hadn't changed in the fifteen years since they parted. He almost hesitated before pressing the remote trigger switch he held in his hand. She screamed as she was suddenly bathed in fire.

Far away in New York, Terry Sawchuk screamed in agony and began to beat at his clothes. The others ran to him, but he'd collapsed on the floor, moaning, crying, and screaming in pain. Tommy was first to reach him, but he was tossed aside. Kylie was next, but Terry shook her off as well. Ella was next and she held him firmly as Harald and Sally drew near. *Be still, Terry. There is no pain. Be still now. Tell us what's happened.*

Even under the compulsion he broke into tears again. "They burned her alive, Ella. They set her on fire and burned her alive. She's dead. Oh dead god, she's dead."

"Terry, be still now, be at peace. We'll bring her back. This I promise you."

"Yes we will," said Harald. "Amanda, you will assist the queen to keep things under control until we return. Terry, where was she?"

"I have that, Sire," said Tommy. "I had her on global positioning."

"Send that position to my phone. Also, I need a plane ready to travel in a hurry."

Eric had been standing in the doorway. He too had strong feelings for the woman he'd known as Ariel, then as Gudrun, and he was deeply loyal to her. "My plane is ready, Sire. I know Stephan Krebs as well as any man. I'll find him for you."

"Then let's go. Terry, Kylie, Ella, you will accompany me. Come, we go to war. I've had enough of this Krebs character.

Vampire Reborn

They were halfway across the Atlantic before anyone spoke. It was Harald who finally broke the silence. Adjusting the headset, he pulled the mike closer to his mouth. "Eric."

"Sire?"

"Can you tell me how it is you come to have a stealth plane that will carry passengers and how you manage to cross borders unchallenged?"

A soft chuckle came from the forward cabin. "Sire, the plane was actually a gift from a secret section of your own government."

"My government?"

"The British. There was no way they could hide a payment of the size they owed us for our successful missions, but they could write off a plane that was not supposed to exist anyway. The plane is stealthed, can carry up to twenty elite troops, and can pass unnoticed anywhere in the world. We often trigger a number of UFO reports, but that's all. Quite useful, don't you think?"

"Indeed I do. So tell me, Eric, how do you plan to find Krebs?"

"I know enough about him to locate the men he'd most likely have used to do this job for him. Once we locate one of them we have a trail to follow. Our team tracker didn't join us, but I expect Kylie will be able to locate him from there."

"You've worked with Gudrun a long time, Eric. You know her skills, how she works. Advise me. What would she do in this case?"

"Tactics isn't my forte, Sire. I'm the procurer; the man who finds the things needed for the mission. We have two professional man hunters with us, Sire. I can find his trail easily enough for them, but I'm not the right one to choose for the tracking."

"Accepted with thanks, Eric. Terry, how are you doing?"

"I've got a hold on it, Harald, I mean Sire. Ella, please take the compulsion off me. I'll need to be able to think clearly for..."

"Of course, Terry. *You are no longer under compulsion, Terry Sawchuk. You are fully in command of your own faculties once again.*"

Tears came to his eyes as the sense of loss and the memory of the pain returned, but he fought it down. Terry had a deeper mission now and he needed to function. He had a man to kill.

"Are you all right, Terry?"

"Yes, Ella, thank you. I should say I'm functional. I'll never be all right again. Not until I've killed that bastard."

Harald's voice was gentle, yet firm as he spoke. "Vengeance is a strong motivator, Terry, but you can't let it rule you."

"I won't Sire, but I want to feel it. I need to feel it."

"So be it, the task of locating Stephan Krebs is yours. We're your assets. Direct us."

Terry squirmed in his seat as he sat up straighter. Shaking off the pain and loss, he forced his training to kick in. "I want Miss Gudrun back. You say you can make that happen. That's your task. Eric, find us a trail then Kylie can take over. As soon as you do that, find us weapons, guns, and lots of them. The bigger the better. Then report to the king to help with whatever he needs to resurrect the lady.

"Sire, you and Ella find and return Miss Gudrun to us. As soon as she's ready I'll hand the task of locating and killing Stephan Krebs over to her. If I haven't killed the son-of-a-bitch already."

Harald nodded his agreement just as Eric spoke. "We're coming in for a landing people. Fasten the safety belts."

"Landing," exclaimed Ella. "There's no runway..."

"This is a British plane, Ma'am," chuckled Eric. "It's modelled on the Harrier concept. All I need is a good sized parking lot like this one."

The plane touched down, then taxied into a large empty warehouse. Eric was first off the plane and speaking with the man who was closing the huge doors. The man nodded then hurried away. A small tour bus soon arrived. They'd had only moments to stretch their legs before they were ushered inside.

The bus headed into Copenhagen with Eric at the wheel. "The bus is armoured and there are small arms beneath your seats. We'll go directly to the location Tommy gave us and proceed from there."

"Just drop us off, Eric," growled Terry, "then find us a trail."

"I'm already on it, Terry. I want this bastard as badly as you do."

"I doubt that."

"Fair to say. She didn't claim me as she did you, but I still want to avenge the closest friend I've ever had. Our people are making inquiries as we speak. By the time we reach the city I should have a name. Once I have a name we'll have a man. That man will have information to share, and I promise you, he will share it."

"Fair enough." Terry nodded and sank back into his own thoughts. Soon they entered the city. Eric drove straight to the warehouse where they expected to find Gudrun's bones. It was empty, but Ella easily caught her scent and the scent of the burnt flesh. "She was here. This is the place, but the bones have been removed."

"Are you certain they weren't reduced to ash?" asked Harald.

"They weren't, Sire. The flames weren't hot enough nor were they focused on her long enough. No, someone's disposed of the remains. There's another scent here, fresher than Gudrun's, but not by much. That'll be the scent of our man."

"He'll be here shortly," said Eric as he reentered the building. He'd disappeared for only a few moments, but he was smiling.

"That was pretty quick," said Terry.

Eric nodded and held up his hand to forestall further questions. "Gudrun's been keeping a discreet eye on some of Krebs' associates over the years. One of those men has been spending a lot of money lately. Our people will deliver him in about a half hour. He'll know where to locate her remains and he may have an idea where Krebs has gone."

"That's good work, Eric," said Terry.

"The lady has built up a loyal network of people all across Europe, Terry. I didn't say what had happened to her, only that she was hunting Krebs and wanted to speak with this man."

"He took her this way," said Ella, as she followed the faint scent. "I could follow more easily as the cat."

"There's no need, Ella," sighed Harald. "He'll have had a vehicle nearby. It's a great sadness to me that the resources and defences that protected us for so long are of little use in an urban environment."

Ella let her shoulders slump. "Sadly, I agree with you, my king. This era is proving much harder to adapt to than any before it."

"But we are adapting, Mother. We're not finished yet, not by a long... Vehicle approaching."

"Mine," grinned Eric. He stepped out through the door then soon returned pushing a shaking man ahead of him. "You'll tell these people what you've done with her body."

"I don't know what you're talking about. What body? Why are you speaking English? What..."

He got no further as Eric hit him hard, sending him crashing to the floor. He tried to regain his feet, but Eric planted a boot on his knee sending him back to the floor, screaming in pain. "Speak before I start having too much fun," growled Eric as he seized the man by the ears and lifted him high into the air. He dropped the screaming body to the floor then kicked him again.

"Eric, there is no need for this. I can get the information from him."

"Understood, Ma'am, but this is the scum who killed Gudrun. I want him to feel pain, fear, and to know he is going to die and why."

"Agreed, Eric, and he will. He'll tell us what we want to know, then he will sacrifice his own life to restore her's."

Eric grinned and backed away. The terrified man gulped then screamed as she grabbed his collar and jerked him off the floor and into the air. "*Be silent and be still.*" Ella dropped him on his feet and he stood still quivering in fear. *"Answer my questions truthfully. Where is the body of the woman you killed?"*

"I put it in a bag and dropped it in the ocean."

"Where is Stephan Krebs?"

"I don't know."

Kylie whispered to Ella and she nodded. *"Where was he?"*

"I don't know."

"Tell me how he contacted you and how you got paid."

"He only contacts by phone, a phone that can't be traced. I picked up my money at the Hilton Hotel near the airport."

"He'll be gone by now," muttered Eric, "but I can find out where he went." He pulled out his phone and began to speak in Danish.

Ella turned back to the captive. *"Take us to the place where you disposed of the body. Eric will drive, you will direct him."* Without a word or a single sign of emotion the man turned and walked to the bus.

The trip took a while but eventually they arrived at an older dock. *"What did you do next?"*

"I stole a boat, rowed out, and dumped her where the men won't fish because the sunken wrecks snag the nets."

"I'll get us a boat," said Eric as he started away. He approached several men who were talking and passing the time. He joined them for a while. Ella was starting to get impatient when she saw money exchange hands and Eric waved them towards a boat plenty big enough to hold them all. They boarded then Eric started the engine.

"So, you're a ship's captain as well."

"Plane, boat, bus, it's all the same, Sire." He grinned as Harald gave him a friendly slap on the shoulder.

Following the controlled man's directions, they manoeuvred out into the harbour. Finally he stopped them. *"This is the place?"*

"Yes."

"What am I looking for?"

"A large black bag made of heavy vinyl; I weighed it down with stone."

Ella swiftly stripped off her clothes and slipped over the side into the waters. She disappeared for several moments. Kylie was beginning to fret when Ella surfaced again. She gulped in several deep breaths then dived again. Nearly an hour had passed with Ella resurfacing further and further from the boat before diving again.

At last a sabre toothed tiger surfaced beside the boat, a heavy bag in its jaws. Harald seized the bag in a powerful hand and hauled it over the side onto the deck. Ella scrambled into the boat to be wrapped in a blanket. She sat shivering while Eric and Harald opened the bag and carefully removed the stones then re-closed the bag.

The boat docked and Harald gently placed the bag in the bus while Eric returned the keys to the owner. He gave him some more money then joined the people at the bus. Ella still had her captive under control. "Where to now?" asked Eric as he climbed behind the wheel again.

"Back to the warehouse where she was killed, "replied Ella. "I want her to be in a somewhat familiar place when she revives."

With a nod, Eric turned the bus around and headed back the way they had come. While Eric closed the huge doors, Ella carefully arranged the charred corpse on the floor then knelt beside the bones. "Ceremony is not necessary, nor is the rearranging of the bones, but it will ease her return. Harald, have you ever done this?"

"Never for another, not in all my long years, Mother."

"Assist me. Just follow my lead."

He nodded and knelt across the body from her. Kylie gasped as Ella gashed her own wrist and let the blood drip on the charred lips of the corpse. "By the blood of the mother. Live again."

Harald nodded then gashed his own wrist, holding it out so the dripping blood would reach her lips. "By the blood of the brother. Live again."

The body stirred slightly and moaned softly. Ella grabbed the arm of her captive, slashing it open with a fang. The blood flowed freely onto Gudrun's hungry lips. "By the blood of the killer. Live again. Rise up my daughter."

Before their very eyes the corpse began to heal its burns and to clothe itself in new flesh. The captive was quivering in terror now, but couldn't move. The compulsion was too strong. Slowly the charred form struggled to its feet with Ella's help. "Mother, I hunger."

"This one took your life, my child." Ella thrust the hapless man into Gudrun's grasp. "He will now return it to you. Drink. Drink long and deep. Heal."

She released the compulsion in time for the man to scream as that charred and disfigured head grew fangs and reached for his throat. He whimpered and struggled weakly for a moment then went limp in her arms. She drank noisily until there was nothing more for him to give. Gudrun dropped the limp body to the floor and wiped her mouth on the back of her hand.

The body on the floor lurched as she kicked it. The memories flooded back as the corpse before her shrivelled to feed her renewing body. Once she was whole again she finally met Ella's eyes then stepped into her arms. "Mother, you brought me back."

"Yes. I have, with Amanda's help, accepted that you all are my children. I will always do my utmost to protect my children. Besides, the world wouldn't be the same without you."

"I'll just bet." She chuckled and hugged Ella fiercely for a moment then released her. "My king, you gave of your life force as well."

"Welcome back, my sister." Harald grinned as he too hugged the tall blonde.

She smiled warmly as she returned the embrace. He released her and she stepped out of his arms to pull Kylie close and hug her too. "It is good to see you too, my sister." Releasing Kylie, she turned to Eric.

"Back from the dead, Gudrun. Now there's a trick worth learning. I thought you might want clothes."

"What, you don't like me naked?"

"No, Terry would kill me for what I'm thinking. Get dressed, save a life."

She laughed with delight as she pulled on the black jumpsuit and stepped into the boots. She tossed back her hair and stepped up to Terry. He hadn't spoken or moved, but there were tears in his eyes and a smile on his face. "And now for you. Terry, this has put you through hell. A hell no one should have to experience.

"I got sloppy and let my guard down. This put you all at risk and caused you all to suffer, my poor Terry most of all. I'm truly sorry for that."

"You're back and okay, that's all that matters, Blondie."

"The hell it is." She reached for him and pulled him into her arms, holding him tightly. "The hell it is, Terry. You're precious to me. I would never have put you through that."

He clung to her tightly and allowed a single sob to escape him. Suddenly her lips were on his, warm and sweet, her body melting against him, so he was forced to hold her up. As their lips parted she kissed his cheek then whispered in his ear. "All better now?"

"Gods, Blondie, you sure have a hell of a way to change a guy's state."

"Works every time," she laughed. "Now put me down. I have a man to find and kill."

"Get in line, Blondie." He reluctantly released his hold on her and allowed her to step back. "This fucker is mine. You're right. I've been through hell in the past twenty-four hours. Krebs will die for that. You stay out of sight. By now he'll have bragged all over Europe about how he killed the greatest merc in history. If you suddenly show up alive they'll all know the wolves aren't the only unusual people around."

"He has a point," said Harald.

She shook her head and reached for Terry's shoulder, giving it a gentle squeeze. "Terry, this man is extremely dangerous. I don't want to risk you against him. You've seen what he's capable of."

"What, you don't think I've got what it takes to face him?"

"That's not it and you know it. It's his organization, Terry. You can't fight them all. If you want to go after him, all right, but please take Eric's sister with you."

"My sister? I have no sister."

"Of course you do." she grinned as she lightly laid her hand on Eric's cheek. She closed her eyes and drew several deep breaths. Terry gasped in amazement as her face altered and her hair darkened. When she opened her eyes they were still that startling blue that he loved, but that was all. "Well, what do you think?"

Eric just shook his head in amazement. "I think my father was a very bad man for cheating on my mother like that." This brought a round of chuckles. "It is good to see you again, Elsa, my sister."

"How about it, Terry. Want a new girlfriend?"

"All right, girl. Just don't let Gudrun find out."

"We'll be very discrete. She'll never suspect a thing."

"All right, people, we have a hunt to conduct. Terry, you have the most experience at this. You take the lead. Find this man."

"Yes, Sire. I'll be more than happy to find him for you. Eric, we'll need the resources and contacts of Miss Gudrun's organization. Will it hold together once the word spreads that she's been killed?"

"That could be a problem."

Terry sighed and thought for a moment. "Kylie, I need you to work your magic."

"Okay, boss, what's our story?"

"A woman was found in a warehouse in Denmark. She was badly burned, but still alive. She's been flown to America for special treatments and is expected to make a full recovery in time. That should hold the organization together for Eric, scare the crap out of Krebs, and allow Miss Gudrun to return to her natural form once this is over."

Harald just grinned. "I like it, Terry. Now, we all need some rest before we go any further with this. Overtired people make mistakes, and we can't afford mistakes against this opponent. Besides, Elsa needs to hunt and then rest. Eric, have we access to a safe house?"

"We do, Sire. Everybody onto the bus. Not you, little sister, you've been naughty. You'll have to find your own way home."

She lightly punched his arm and grinned. "Station six?"

"Station Six." He nodded then climbed aboard the bus and drove away. Gudrun went hunting.

Chasing the Dream

While the tourists and local sunbathers enjoyed the perfect day on the beaches of the blue Mediterranean Sea, one man sat gazing from his hotel window. Lost in thought and concerned. He was too close now, far too close for this to be allowed to happen. Stephan Krebs sighed then took another sip of the expensive cognac, his one true vice.

"Why now, Ariel, why did you come to me now? A task for me? Truly? A trap for me is more likely. Yes, you would have lured me into a trap, but for who? Who has the kind of money to tempt you to come after me? Who would dare?"

Who indeed? Stephan Krebs was nearing his goal of controlling all crime of consequence in the world. Already his people were tearing down the government of America. That was key to his plan to bring peace to the world. Bring down all the governments who could challenge him, bring them under his control. He had been extremely successful in America over the past ten years or more. Britain wasn't so far behind.

Stephan took another look at the sunbathers in the distance and snorted in derision then tossed back the cognac. His father had said it best. It was all he could remember of the man, his favourite saying. "The criminals control everything." And it rang true. So, it naturally followed that if you want to bring peace to the world, you had to gain control of the criminals. Everywhere. He was drawing close to achieving that aim, and it was few indeed who knew it, or who it was pulling the strings.

"Why now, Ariel?" He sighed again and poured another glass. Who could have sent her, and he not have known? "It has to be one of the American drug cartels. There are only three beyond my control.

70

Had Ariel not interfered there would be only one left. A minor irritant at best, but now?" He shook his head and began to pace about the room. "An example will have to be made, but which one? Inquiries must be made.

"Without Ariel, her mercenaries will fall apart and seek out other work. They are no longer a problem. Perhaps I'll make an example of them all, just to be certain I have the right one." That thought brought a smile to his face. The glass made its way back to his lips.

That cold smile was still on his lips as the empty glass returned to the table. His father might actually have been proud of him, if he knew. His father would get his peace. Stephan had been a boy when his father had thrown him out of the house, screaming that he would have some peace if it was the last thing he would ever do. Stephan would bring him that peace, world peace, then he would find him and grant him final peace.

THE CONSTANT HUM OF the plane's engines had Stephan lulled to a half sleep. In spite of himself, his thoughts returned to the magnificent woman he had recently killed. Of all the lives he had ended, this was the one he regretted. She had been compelling as well as beautiful. "Oh Ariel, it could have been so different. Why were you so intent on staying on the right side of the law, as you put it?"

She'd had no real ambition; that had been the problem. He had often urged her to join him in his plan to rule the world, to bring peace to the many war-ravaged lands of the planet. She only laughed and said it would put her out of work. She'd had no plan, no vision for the future, just live for the day and enjoy. That was her motto.

It certainly wasn't his. He'd been a victim much of his young life. Violence at home, on the streets, then in the military. Ariel had tried to show him a different way. Her way. He knew the difference. To see change, you had to bring change, violent and abrupt change. Change would only come through violence and pain. He'd learned to be very good at both.

"Ah Ariel, if only you could have seen the truth, understood, then I wouldn't have had to kill you."

"But you did kill me." In his sleepy state her face suddenly appeared before him. Accusing, challenging, threatening. "You took my life, Stephan. Now I will take yours. It's only a matter of time until I catch you." The face moved closer and changed as fangs grew from the jaws.

He jerked awake, sitting bolt upright with a startled gasp. Disoriented, he glanced about, searching for her, for the ghost.

"Are you all right, sir?"

"What? Oh yes, I'm fine. Just startled awake, that's all."

"Can I get you a pillow?"

"No, I'll be fine, thank you."

He sighed and settled back as she walked away. "I don't believe in ghosts, Ariel. However, I do believe in revenge. I wonder, will your merry band of mercenaries hold together now that you're gone? I doubt it. No, I'm finished with that threat forever."

To take his mind off that line of thought, he pulled out his phone and began to peruse the news headlines. Suddenly he sat bolt upright, adrenaline coursing through his system. A woman was found badly burned, but still alive.

No, it couldn't be her. It couldn't. Could it? There was no name given for the woman, but it had to be her. He had to believe it was her. A full recovery? No! Could that be possible? She would come for him now. Once recovered, she would come, and she would come for blood.

Wide awake now, with thoughts racing, he turned to face the window, gazing at the darkness outside. "No, stay on track. Keep your focus on the mission. The deed will be done long before she can completely recover. There's still time, but we must speed up the timetable.

"I'll send Marco to find her in America. Perhaps he can eliminate that threat before it matures. Marco has never failed me, and he won't fail this time. She will die there in a hospital bed, wrapped in bandages..."

It was two days and three countries later when Stephan learned someone was on his trail. An American CIA agent or something. Why? Who was this unknown man? A few phone calls and Stephan had his answer. The man was a former agent who had been last seen in the company of a tall blonde woman. Ariel, or Gudrun as she had called herself.

So, she had taken a lover after all. A jealous rage leaped up in Stephan's heart, but he fought it back. No, that was the way to certain death. If her lover was so intent on catching him, perhaps that should be arranged. Killing this foolish hunter would be good practice for the wolf cubs.

Yes, but the trail can't be too easy to follow, he might suspect. This could be entertaining, and should Marco fail to find her, Ariel would recover to learn of her lover's death. Stephan smiled to himself at the thought. Surely that would drive her to make another mistake. This one would be her last.

Picking Up The Trail

The vampires were all asleep as Kylie slipped silently through the big old house. They were all accustomed to her scent now and her movements didn't disturb them. She found Eric in the kitchen enjoying a cup of coffee and staring at his phone.

"So, a fellow morning person I see. Is there any more of that coffee?"

"The pot's there, Kylie." He smiled, pointing to the coffee pot. "Mugs are in the cupboard above it."

"Have you seen Terry?"

"No, but I believe I heard a taxi pull up outside then drive away. It must have been him."

"Dammit, he's gone hunting." With a sigh and a sip of the coffee, she sank gracefully into a chair facing him. "He gets like this when the trail's cold. He could be gone for days."

"Did you find out where Stephan has gone?"

"Yes and no. I know where he went from here, but I doubt that was his real destination."

"You'll be quite right there. Stephan's like a fox. He has several dens in which to hide, but I'm sure that, in the years since we last saw him, he's acquired a few more. He changes them up constantly."

"Sounds like a smart boy."

"He is, frighteningly so, and Ariel trained him well."

"Ariel, you mean Gudrun?"

"Yes. She was called Ariel then. Stephan had a wild crush on her, but she wouldn't have him. He left us in anger when she finally told him to shut up about his big plan to rule the world."

"Plan to rule the world?"

"He believes that by controlling all major crime in the world he can control everything. He said it was the only way to bring world peace. Through violence. Governments are too hesitant about the violence needed to bring peace, therefore it must be accomplished through the crime lords.

"I can still hear him saying that. With so much conviction, begging Ariel to join him in the quest. She told him to shut up about it or leave. He left."

"Shit, a bloody-minded zealot." Another sigh followed by a bigger sip from the coffee mug.

Eric pushed away the phone and leaned back in the chair. "That disturbs you?"

"It does, Eric. A criminal, a brutal man, or a man driven by passions he can't control is a lot easier to find. A zealot will be far more determined, and will likely have gathered more like himself around him. People who believe the dream. This will make him a lot harder to find and harder to bring down."

"I see. You could be right about that."

"She is right about that." Gudrun yawned and then smiled. She was back to her natural form. She poured a coffee for herself then joined them at the table. "What?"

Eric just grinned and shook his head. "In the past year I've seen things that would drive most men completely mad. Somehow it doesn't seem to bother me like you'd expect. Gudrun, did you use that compulsion thing on me?"

"Of course I did. You asked me to, remember."

"Oh yes, so I did. Thank you for that. I've always been afraid of ghosts. Seeing you walk in here like this would surely have made me faint dead away otherwise."

"Always the joker when things get tense, Eric." She reached for his phone and pushed it back toward him. "What did you learn?"

Eric sighed and leaned his elbows on the table, not making eye contact with her or Kylie. "Melos is dead. Murdered last night."

"What? Warn the other..."

"Already done, Gudrun. Everyone has gone to ground. All have been warned to choose new places to hide. None of the old standards are to be used."

"But aren't we in..."

"Yes we are, Kylie." Gudrun grinned wickedly. "Eric wasn't awake early, he never slept. He was hoping some of Stephan's men would show up here for me to question. Am I right, Eric, old friend?"

"As always, Gudrun. It was too much to hope for, but we needed a place to rest, and I thought it was worth a shot."

"So, where's Terry? I thought he'd be part of your little trap."

"He left as soon as you fell asleep."

Gudrun tilted her head slightly as though listening, her eyes focused far away. "He's hunting, and somewhat pleased with himself. However, I'm concerned at the levels of rage in him. He's controlling it well, but..."

"You were killed by fire, Gudrun," Kylie said, lightly patting her hand. "Terry felt it and he felt you die. He worships you, Gudrun, and he did before you marked him. He knows that as soon as our killer learns he failed he'll try again."

Gudrun sighed and studied her hands. "I know, Kylie, I know. I wouldn't have put him through that, I wouldn't. It's been centuries since I've allowed myself to love anyone. Oh yes, I've taken lovers. Plenty of them. But I didn't love them as I did my Igor so long ago. The pain of watching him grow old and die was unbearable to me."

"I sense a *but* in there."

"Yes, Kylie, there is one. But this time it sneaked up on me. Terry is so... solid, I guess is the word. Like an anchor I can hold to, a wall to lean on."

"Planning to tell him sometime this century?"

"Yes, when the time is right I'll tell him, but not yet."

"Why not yet?"

"Because, Kylie, right now he sees me as a child that needs to be protected. That will only get him killed and I want him to live. No, once he starts to see me as the powerful vampire as he did before, when his confidence in me has been restored, then I'll tell him."

"Gudrun, he has every confidence in you."

"Confidence in my ability to defend myself, Kylie. I made a mistake. I underestimated Stephan's caution, and his willingness to sacrifice everything for his cause."

"Everybody makes mistakes. Terry knows that."

"Yes, but he needs to have his confidence in my ability to make quality decisions restored."

"He needs that, or you need it?"

"Has Ella never warned you about how dangerous it can be to torment a vampire? Yes, Mother Kylie, I need to restore my confidence in myself before I can go to him. I won't present him with a less than whole woman to stand beside him. What is it, Eric?"

"Nothing, nothing at all." Her glower caused him to chuckle and sit back in his chair, hands raised protectively. "It's just I've never seen you all love struck before. It's kind of..."

"If you say cute, I swear I will bite your head off."

He rose easily from the chair. "I think I should go see if the bus needs fuel." He was still chuckling as he disappeared through the door.

"You see what I mean, Kylie? One little death by fire and the men lose all respect for you."

"Joke all you want, Blondie, but you scared the crap out of us all. Besides, that man loves you, too."

"I know he does. I worked very hard to bring that round to brotherly love, Kylie. I'm extremely fond of Eric."

"But he doesn't start your engine."

"It's not that. When you go into battle with people, you need to all be brothers in arms. A lover will try to protect you instead of doing his own job, petty jealousies can arise within the crew, etc."

"So you shut it down with Eric, but not with Terry. Why?"

"I did try, but there's just something about that guy."

"Oh girl, you've got it bad," laughed Kylie.

"He's coming back. Kylie, if you..."

"Lips are sealed, girl. This one is yours to figure out."

Terry came through the door, sniffing the air like a hunting hound. "Is that coffee I smell?" He stopped and looked long and lovingly at Gudrun, then snapped out of it as Kylie passed him a mug of coffee. "Good morning, Miss Gudrun. You have no idea how nice it is to see you again."

Gudrun drank in the sight of him, the kind of man she was always drawn to physically. Terry was barely five foot six, but well over a two hundred pounds of hardened muscle. Without his standard government suit, his regular street clothes showed off the muscle and she liked that, too. Better yet, she got a sweet thrill from the way he always looked at her.

"Really, Terry? From what I hear you've been seeing another woman instead of saving yourself for me."

"You mean Elsa, Eric's sister? Yes, well, she is pretty cute, but way too young for me."

"Is that so? Are you saying I'm old?"

Terry blushed and studied his coffee. "Kylie, quick, change the subject."

"I should let you hang for leaving without telling me, but, all right. Terry, did you learn anything?"

"Yeah, I learned some interesting things, but not the location of that bastard."

Gudrun shifted to warrior mode instantly. She was once again the mercenary troop leader. "Report, what did you learn?"

He grinned with pleasure as she returned to the woman he had fallen for the instant he'd first seen her. "I found I have a friend in this city, an old acquaintance from Interpol. He told me they've been trying to track this guy for years. Krebs owns property in a dozen countries. He's rarely seen at any of them, but he's occasionally seen at places owned by shell companies he owns.

"He's taken control of most of the organized crime in Europe and Asia, but there's no way to prove any of this. Krebs has a fondness for the good life, he's addicted to a certain brand of cognac..."

"Cognac Park."

"That's it. My friend also gave me the name of a local man I might want to meet."

Gudrun smiled and tapped his wrist with a delicate finger. "Is that why your knuckles are bruised?"

"Yes, well, I had to teach the man to speak English. Since I can't put the compulsion on anyone, I had to do it the old fashioned way."

"Did he learn English?"

"He did. He told me that Krebs has a tendency to be too organized in the way he changes up his travels. He believed our boy would be in Spain using the name Collard."

"Son of a bitch," snarled Kylie as she retrieved her laptop and returned to the table. "I'll bet he has a different name for every country he enters."

"He does," sighed Terry, as he sat back in the chair, cradling the coffee mug in both hands. "He changes them up every six months regular as clockwork. The next change is due this week."

"He'll also be changing his appearance," sighed Gudrun. "He'll have something new for each country. A cane, white hair, a false scar, glasses, different style of clothes, that sort of thing."

"That won't help him," muttered Kylie. "He can run, but he can't hide forever, not from me. What else have you got, Terry? This man can't control half the crime syndicates in the world without help."

"His right hand man is a badass named Marco Bueno. Apparently the guy is one tough son of a bitch. As far as my friend knew, this Marco is Krebs' go to guy. The one he'll trust above all others."

"So, are you thinking what I'm thinking?"

"Oh yeah. I sure as hell am."

"Would you care to enlighten me, kiddies?" said Gudrun.

"Miss Gudrun, we put the word out that you survived and were being shipped to America for burn treatments."

"Yes, so?"

"If this Marco is Krebs' *go to* guy, Krebs will most likely send him to find and kill you. If we can peg him off, you can put the compulsion on him, and he'll take us right to the target."

"I love the way you two think." Gudrun smiled, well pleased with this turn of events. "So, if Marco heads for the U.S. how do we find him there?"

"He'll be looking for a badly burned woman," replied Kylie, her fingers flying across her keyboard. "My first choice would be the John Hopkins Centre, it's the best known in the world. Have you got a description for me, Terry?"

"Big guy, tall like Krebs, maybe six-two or better. Lots of muscle, scar on right cheek, dark complexion, black hair, going bald, moustache, no beard, brown eyes, full sleeve tattoos, gold tooth on the right upper as you look at him."

"So, what's the plan?"

"I don't want to go chasing after him, Kylie..."

Terry stopped speaking as Gudrun reached across the table to squeeze his shoulder and lock her penetrating gaze on him. "If you're thinking of sending me back to the U.S. after this man while you stay here to track Stephan Krebs..."

Terry sighed and let his gaze drop. "Busted. I was hoping Harald would go with you..."

"Terry, I let my guard down for a moment. I didn't realize he'd become even more cautious over the passing years. However, that doesn't mean I need to be coddled or protected like a child. We have people there who can intercept him. I know Gina would truly enjoy getting the information out of him. Terry, your job is to find him. Let the vampires take care of the rest."

With a sigh he brought his gaze back to meet hers. "All right, here's the deal, Blondie. Nobody gets put on the shelf on this one. We go at this bastard together. Deal?"

She gave him that smile that nearly melted his knees. "Deal, my friend. We'll take him down together."

Ella walked in with Harald at this point. Terry began to make up a fresh pot of coffee as they gathered round the table. Eric returned and Kylie swiftly brought them up to speed.

Harald nodded as he absorbed all the new information. "So, we have a battle plan. Now we wait until Kylie or Tommy gets a lead on this Marco character. Perhaps I'll check in on Sally to see how things are going on the home front."

Teaching Old Wolves New Tricks Isn't Easy

On the home front, Sally wasn't having as much fun as Harald, in fact, she wasn't having any fun at all. She was ready to tear her hair out. Since the shapeshifters arrived she'd been petitioned by one after the other. "Is my child still alive? Is she safe? Is she harmed? Are they feeding them? Are they torturing them?" Sally was at a loss. She was almost ready to ask one of the vampires to put a compulsion on them all.

Sally got to her feet and began to pace. Muttering to herself, she tried to find a solution. Dammit, humans had skills. She had to show these vampires that the humans were their equals in many ways. She had to bring comfort to the shapeshifters as well. If Terry Sawchuk were here she could have put him in charge then... oh yeah, there's the answer. She turned back and sat to the queen's throne, as Harald called her favourite chair at the long meeting table.

"Tommy, call everyone here, vampire and shapeshifter."

"Yes, ma'am." His fingers flew and phones began to ring across the city. In less than an hour the room was filled. The humans and vampires were curious, the shapeshifters shy and nervous. "Looks like everyone is here, Sally."

"Thank you, Tommy. People, we're in the midst of mass confusion here. We have no time for this, not now."

"My queen, what have you learned?" asked Gina.

Before Sally could answer Tommy passed her a sheet of paper, still warm from the printer. She read it carefully then looked up. "We need to get organized and swiftly. Gina, perhaps this is a task for you." She passed the note over to the small woman whose smile began to broaden as she read it.

82

"Yes, my queen. I believe this is indeed a task for me."

"That man will have the location of the children as well as the man responsible for so much death. Do you need any help?"

"No, my lady, I believe I can deal with this Marco. I'll intercept him and get that location for you."

"The instant you know, contact Harald."

"Yes, my queen, it shall be as you desire. I go." With that she fairly danced from the room.

Sally faced the gathered folk. "That message was from Kylie. She's discovered that Stephan Krebs' right hand man will be on his way to America, or so we believe. Gina will intercept him and get the location of your pups from him. We'll soon be one large step closer to our goal.

"What can we do to help?" asked Illya.

"Frankly, sir, you can stop fighting our people and learn what they're trying to teach you."

"It is all too confusing, Great Queen. So many buttons to push, things on screens that move too fast, machines, carriages, the language so difficult, and the noise, the noise..."

"Enough," sighed Sally. "You're Illya, aren't you. Come sit beside me, Illya, and listen carefully." The room was silent as he approached and sat. For some reason he was more frightened by her than he was by the vampires.

Sally took his hands and let her vision blur for a moment. When she released him her eyes hardened. "What did you see, Great Queen?"

"Illya, the time will come, and soon, when you will all be called upon to fight for your children. Tommy, as soon as we're finished here I'll call Harald. For now, I need you to organize us."

"Me?"

"You. Tommy, you're the most efficient and organized person I know. Organize us, please."

"Well, okay, if you say so. We need to work fast. Language is a big part of the problem. I suggest..."

"Don't suggest, Tommy. Command."

"Yes, ma'am. Okay, people, Miss Gudrun has been returned to us, and a story put out about her surviving the fire but being sent to America for treatment. Krebs' assassin, a man named Marco, will likely be on his way. Miss Gina has already left for the most likely place for him to show up. She'll deal with him. All other vampires keep cruising the streets near here. Make sure no one suspects anything, or if they do, they forget it forever.

"Vassily and Jimmy are the only combat trained troops we have. They will remain inside the building complex and provide security. Georg and Olla have been in North America the longest, so they have the best command of the language. They also have the best understanding of the technology and know how to function in our society. They will work with Amanda and Clyde to help teach the others.

"They can also work with me to help get the folk ready as quickly as possible."

"And what of me, Tommy?"

"Ma'am?"

"What should I be doing?"

"Can we speak privately?"

"Of course. If that's all, then get to it, folks." The room slowly emptied out then she turned back to Tommy. "All right, Tommy, talk to me."

"Yes, ma'am."

"We're in private, Tommy. Sally is fine."

"Sorry, Sal. Look, you're the queen. The queen doesn't work beside the others. To retain the level of awe and respect you need you'll have to remain somewhat aloof."

"Dammit, Tommy, I need to be doing something."

"And you are, Sal. You took control, explained the situation, set me in charge of accomplishing the tasks at hand. Now you're supposed to show up once in a while, frown at the slow pace of progress, and encourage us to pick up some speed."

"You seem to have quite a store of knowledge on this sort of thing, Tommy."

"I read a lot."

"Sure."

"Okay, I'm addicted to fantasy novels. Happy now?"

She grinned with delight at his blush of embarrassment. "Delighted. Do you play video games as well."

"Not so much anymore. It's way too easy for folks to get information from you during a game. Ever since I joined the original team I've stuck to the novels."

"That's good thinking, Tommy. So, you've got a thing for Olla."

"What? How the hell did you come to that conclusion?"

"I'm psychic, remember?" Sally laughed as he blushed. "Also, you don't hide it very well."

"Shit. Do you think she noticed anything?"

"I'm sure of it."

"Oh damn." He sighed, blushing even deeper.

"Why Olla, Tommy? I've never heard you mention a woman before...or a man either."

"It just didn't make sense to allow myself that kind of a fantasy." He shook his head and sank into the chair beside her.

"You know the level of secrecy we worked under with the government. Now it's even tighter. Olla is very pretty, smart, and far too sad. I just want to take her in my arms and protect her, but I know she can shift into a dire wolf and kill with ease."

"Yes, she could, but that doesn't mean she would. However, I do understand the uneven playing field in the physical department. I'm sure there's more. Keep talking."

Tommy grinned and looked away shyly. "Well, it seems to me there'd be a lot less secrecy, you know, if we became a couple. I know what she is and what she's done. I also know why. I'd have done the same if it were me. She knows what I do for a living and I won't need to worry about exposing a secret. Ah well, it doesn't matter anyway. She'd never look at a mere human. But it's a nice dream."

Standing just outside the door waiting, Olla blushed. This man, so important to the queen and king. How could he want such as her? A killer. A freak of nature. It had been less than a year since she'd watched helplessly as her mate was killed. It seemed longer somehow.

Her world had changed a lot since that day. The time of innocence in the mountains was past. The modern world had found them, hunted them, captured them, and forced them to do terrible things. Tommy knew. He knew all about that, yet he was interested. He seemed nice, gentle, and kind. Could he give her more pups? She wondered if his people and hers could mate successfully. Perhaps she would find out. Olla blushed again and moved away from the door as she heard him coming.

THE DAY HAD BEEN LONG, but it had finally wound down. Sally was actually grateful that the shapeshifters weren't nocturnal like the vampires. That little thing actually made things a bit easier. She smiled as she watched Clyde, Clara, and Amanda say their good nights to the wolf people.

With Olla and Georg working with them as interpreters things had gone rather smoothly. Their greater comfort with the English language and technology of the modern world made all the difference. The shapeshifters no longer felt like they were being forced into a new mold, but rather being helped by their own to learn how to survive in this strange world.

Sally smiled with delight as Georg watched Clara walk to the door. Her smile broadened as Clara glanced back with a shy smile before stepping through. Soon only Olla was left in the reception area. Sally made eye contact then pointed to the light still on in Tommy's office. Olla's eyes widened as the queen smiled and turned back towards her own chambers.

Olla stood motionless, watching Sally go. "She approves. If so, the king's approval should not be hard to win. Now, perhaps it's time for me to see if I could enjoy this man. He's not the alpha, but he is well respected in this pack. They say they'll get my pups back and they will need a father. Could this man be a father for wolves? Ah well, standing here will bring no answers." Squaring her shoulders, she approached the door to his office and tapped gently.

"It's open," he called, his back to the door and his eyes fixed on the screen. "I'm just...Olla, hi." He smiled and blushed shyly.

She liked that. She returned his smile and stepped closer. "You work late, Mr. Tommy. You always work so late. I wondered what magic you do here, alone at night."

"Tommy. Just Tommy, please, Olla. Come here. I'll show you what I'm doing. Stephan Krebs controls several crime syndicates. It took me a while to discover which ones, but I tracked down a few. Here's that short list." Tommy popped a list up on the screen.

"Now, over here is the real work. I hacked into each of the organizations and gathered what information I could. Names, addresses, who answers to who. I'm searching for the chain of command that leads up to Krebs. I want to find out who's high ranking enough to know his whereabouts.

"This computer is organizing all the information I've gathered, looking for commonalities, overlaps, ... This is boring as shit, isn't it."

"This shit is not boring," she mused. "It's just difficult to understand. So, first you find the people who don't want to be found. You then enter their lair, so to speak, and steal what you want. Now you try to make sense of it in a way that will help us locate the children. You don't believe Miss Gina will succeed?"

"We don't know for certain if that man will come. It's only a guess. If she calls tomorrow with the information I'll abandon this, but for now I must continue. As I gather information, I send it to Kylie to help her track the man down."

Olla sighed and stepped even closer. Tommy could reach out and touch her if he chose to do so. He truly wanted to. She sighed again. "So, just as I'm a killer, you're a thief. Is this correct?"

She watched him carefully for his reaction. He stiffened for a split second then relaxed again. "Well, that's one way to put it, but it's far too simplistic." His voice was soft and gentle as he reached out to take hold of her shoulders. "You're more than a killer, Olla."

"What am I then, Tommy?" She didn't reject his touch. She was actually pleased that her body enjoyed the touch. Her mind as well.

Gently he pulled her closer, into his personal space. She felt no resistance as she stepped closer to him. Another good sign. "You became a killer because you had no choice. You're also a mother, and a woman with a quick mind. You're also quite beautiful."

"I shed."

"What???"

"I often sleep in wolf form. It's easier to fall asleep, for the wolf feels no remorse at the killing. I shed."

A slow mischievous smile spread over his boyish features. "That's okay, I'm not allergic."

"What???"

"It won't make me sneeze if you shed."

"Let me go." Olla pushed gently against his chest. His arms opened and she stepped back. Another test passed. He had a gentle sense of humour, and he wouldn't force her. Now for the big test. She began to strip off her clothes.

Somewhat bewildered by her sudden change of mood and odd behaviour, Tommy started to turn away, but she stopped him. "No, do not avert your eyes. You must see this. I must know." He was feasting his eyes on the gloriously naked woman just out of his reach when she suddenly shimmered into a huge wolf with glowing eyes.

To his credit, Tommy didn't panic and run, nor did he take a single step back as the wolf approached. The wolf stepped closer and sniffed him all over, the tail slowly waving from side to side.

Finally the muzzle slipped into his hand and flipped his arm into the air. The beast rose up on its hind legs and rested its paws on his shoulders. It licked his face then shimmered back into a naked Olla whose arms were around his neck. She let her eyes flutter closed as he tightened his arms around her and kissed her.

Olla felt her desire stir even as she felt his manhood surge to life against her belly. Another test passed. He didn't flinch from the wolf and it was obvious he still wanted her. "Tommy, now you've seen what I am. Can you truly want this?"

"I've wanted you from the moment I saw you. And now my little friend confirms that decision."

"Really?" She slipped her hand down the front of his jeans and gripped him firmly, causing him to groan with delight. "I think perhaps your little friend is not so little."

"Yes, well, that's all your fault."

"My fault? I see. So it becomes my problem to deal with?"

"Oh yeah. Just don't bite it off."

She chuckled as she began to stroke him slowly. "I promise I won't even leave a mark."

She started to slide down his body, but he pulled her back up. "Come back here. I want to kiss you again." He locked his mouth on hers, claiming her, demanding her, aching for the taste of her. Olla's desire rose with a fire she hadn't felt in a long time. She had feared it was gone forever. Suddenly he scooped her into his arms and carried her to the small cot he often slept on, surprising her with his strength.

Tommy lowered her to the bed then, with trembling hands began to fight his way out of his clothes. She rose to her feet with a liquid grace. "Stop now. Let me. After all, it's my task to solve the problem, is it not?"

She swiftly undressed him, then pushed him onto his back on the bed and mounted him. Tommy moaned with the sweet torturous delight as her body slowly engulfed him. His hands found her firm breasts and the bullet hard nipples as she leaned forward for another kiss. "I know how this is for the men, Tommy. Take what you need. We will rest then and after a rest we will enjoy each other at our leisure. Take what you need."

"All right, but no shedding until afterwards."

"Beast," she laughed, as she rose up then settled back down on him. "Now you pay for teasing me." She rose up again then plunged back down. His hands found her butt cheeks and held her tight as he began to thrust up into her. She was amazed when he managed to hold himself back to wait for her. She felt the passion rise deep within her and she quickened her pace. Suddenly her world dissolved into stardust, and she collapsed on his chest as he exploded within her. "So," she panted. "Can I shed now?"

He laughed and hugged her gently. "You can do whatever you like, just promise to stay with me forever."

"Are you so certain? You know wolves mate for life..."

"I'm certain, Olla. Stay with me. Be mine and I'll be yours."

Another test passed for both of them. "As you wish, my Tommy. I'm yours now."

"Then my life is blessed, and I'm the luckiest man in the world." He gently kissed her lips then cuddled her close. Somehow he seemed to understand that cuddling was a true part of her nature and something she would need plenty of. He didn't mind at all. He kissed her again then drifted off to sleep.

Tommy awakened early to find himself alone in the bed. Startled, he sat up and looked all around, wide awake now. There on the floor, sleeping on a pile of his clothes, lay the she wolf. "So, you just had to shed on my clothes, didn't you?" He was grinning and her tail thumped on the floor. She rolled on her back and presented her belly for rubbing. Chuckling with delight, Tommy obliged.

They stepped out of Tommy's office hand in hand. Then Olla's world fell apart. Illya and Anna were waiting for them. "Olla, what have you done?" Olla seemed to shrink in fear and averted her eyes. Bewildered, Tommy stepped in front of her.

Illya went nose to nose with Tommy. "So, you young pup, you wish to challenge me for dominance?"

Tommy swallowed hard, fear written on his face, but he didn't back down. "No, I don't," he replied. "Mind telling me what crawled up your shorts and died?"

"I mated without the alpha's permission, dear Tommy." Olla stepped out from behind him and faced Illya defiantly. "I am no longer of your pack, Illya. Look around you. Where are you? Your pack and the remnants of three others are all here. Safe by the permission of the queen.

"Look behind you. There are three vampires already changed to killing form, and two humans heavily armed with modern weapons aimed at you.

"Illya, the world as we know it has changed. Here, in this place, Queen Sally is the alpha female. I fully believed I had her permission."

"You did and still do have my permission, Olla." Sally appeared, moving slowly across the room with a regal air. Illya could sense nervousness in her, but he was suddenly unsure. "Among Tommy's people no such permission is required."

Illya relaxed his posture slightly as she neared. He had reacted as the alpha, but it was suddenly quite clear he no longer was. "I had already chosen another for her, Great Queen. If our people are to survive, we must produce as many pups as possible. Even if your king recovers those pups who survive, they will not be enough. Olla must mate with her own species."

"Not gonna happen," said Tommy. He was prepared to fight if he had to. It proved unnecessary.

"Actually, that's not true." The voice belonged to Clara Bynes. She pushed her way through the gathered shapeshifters.

"Talk to me, Clara," smiled Sally.

"Well, I've been doing some DNA testing, just out of curiosity you understand."

"Of course." Sally was grinning now and the tension was easing. "Have you drawn any conclusions on the subject that might help us right now?"

"Well, yes I have. The DNA is compatible, so procreation between humans and werewolves is definitely possible. The wolf-shapeshifter gene is quite dominant, so it is more likely any children would be shifters.

"It's my opinion this isn't recommended. The children would grow too fast and be a danger to the human parent. However, if the human parent would consent to the children being raised by the pack of the shifter parent, it could work. However, in that case there would be humans who are aware of the shapshifters. There would be a need for trust between the two just as there's a bond of trust between our group and the vampires."

Sally nodded, and, smiling brightly, turned to Illya. "Satisfied?"

"My feelings no longer matter, Great Queen. You've made your decision. Olla is of your pack now. When we are permitted to leave here, she will remain with her mate. It is done. My pack, those few who remain, will choose another to lead them. I'm finished." Sally's heart broke for him. She had not wanted this.

Georg stepped forward. "Illya, you're a wise and good leader. We both know that, of those who remain, I'm the strongest. None may challenge for leader unless they defeat me first. I expect it'll be one of the pups several years from now who will manage that."

"Georg..."

"Fine, then I challenge." He grabbed the older man by the collar and tried to yank him off his feet.

With a twist and a heave Illya tossed Georg through the air. Georg ended up on his back, the old man kneeling on his chest, a hand gripping his throat. Georg was laughing. "Not so old and weak after all, are you Illya?"

"Stop this," chided Anna. "Stop this right now. You're acting like half starved dogs. Georg, remember your place. Illya, stop sulking. Olla's not the first female to leave the pack for a mate. We must remember why we're here. We must learn all we can as swiftly as we can if we're going to recover our young."

Illya got to his feet then offered his hand and helped Georg to his feet. "You young fool." He gave the younger man a friendly cuff on the ear then turned back to Tommy. Georg winked at Clara who tried and failed to hide her blush.

"Anna is right, Mr. Tommy. I was wrong. You're not of my pack'; you did not challenge me. You did claim a mate and were willing to fight for her. It's as it should be. There's much about our kind that you don't know. I hope you never regret your decision."

"It's all right, I'm not allergic," grinned Tommy.

"What does this mean?"

"I know she sheds, but it doesn't make me sneeze."

Illya grinned in spite of himself. "Young fool. Perhaps you're a match for her after all. Come then, let us learn more of your machines that make beeps and buzz."

Sally sighed with relief as the vampires shifted back to full human and the security guards returned to their rounds. As she headed back to her rooms her phone rang. "Harald? Oh, thank god. No, no, everything is under control...for the moment. Let me bring you up to speed."

A Costly Mistake

Another three days of travel and he was in Scotland. As he drove along, Stephan Krebs thumbed on his phone. His call was answered on the third ring. "Marco."

"Is everything in place?"

"Yes, Stephan, all is as it should be. We arrived unnoticed and are fully ensconced in the old castle. I truly wish we could have chosen somewhere with a better climate. This constant dampness chills me right to the bone, and the woolens to keep it at bay are itchy."

Krebs laughed at that. Marco was the only one who could make him laugh like that. "Alas, poor Marco. I have a task for you, old friend. Perhaps the climate in America would be more to your liking."

"America? What's happened, Stephan?" Marco was all business now.

"It seems I've made a small error. I thought I had killed Ariel, but somehow she has survived the fire. She's been flown to America for treatment for her burns. I don't know where in America, but you should have no trouble tracking her down."

"Have you a current picture?"

"No, Marco. It would be of little use anyway. She was too badly burned to be recognizable."

"But you still consider her a problem?"

"I do. I know her, Marco. If she's alive she will come for me eventually, and when she does, she will come hard and fast. No, I caught her by surprise and thought I had it resolved, but she survived. She must not be allowed to recover. Go to America, find her and kill her."

"She will probably be at their John Hopkins. I'll start the search there. I seek a woman who was brought from Denmark with full body burns, correct?"

94

"Correct. Marco, take no chances. This woman is dangerous."

"I won't fail you, Stephan."

"You never do, old friend. I feel better already."

As Stephan Krebs drove north, Marco packed a light bag. He looked at his favourite gun then tossed it aside. He wouldn't need it and he would be less likely to run into trouble at the American border without it. "Such a paranoid people, those Americans. Ah well, guns are easily acquired there." He finished packing, left word to expect Stephan later that night, then went on his way.

As he drove, Marco worked the current situation over in his mind. Stephan's paranoia concerning this woman was becoming a concern. For whatever reason, this woman had unhinged his mentor. Perhaps it truly was time to seek out other options. Marco was a natural survivor. He had never actually bought into Stephan's crusade. He'd just been trying to keep a secure job. Now that job wasn't looking quite so secure.

By the time Stephan arrived, Marco was passing Loch Lomond on his way to the Glasgow airport.

The island Stephan called his was actually only an island at high tide. At low tide it was accessible, barely, via a rocky beach. It consisted of a few acres of open rocky fields and a low-lying bowl of land filled with pine forest, planted by the former owner. Overlooking the whole thing was the remains of an old castle.

The former owner had upgraded that, too. Stephan had added his own touch to it. The castle now contained a well-appointed living area, several more small cabins, an array of outbuildings, as well as security and defensive systems. The only real approach was the causeway. He'd even had the drawbridge rebuilt.

He smiled as his car rolled down the hill, across that bridge, and into the compound. He felt safe at last. Tossing the keys on a desk just inside the door to his office, Stephan headed for the security cameras. All was quiet.

"Dammit, Ariel. You lie on a bed, no more than an overdone steak from a barbecue, and yet you haunt me. Frighten me. I've taken every possible precaution on my way here, and yet I feel that twitch between my shoulders saying I'm being hunted, tracked." Nervously he poured himself a shot of his favourite cognac. Damn the woman anyway. Why had she come? Who? Who could have hired her, set her on his trail?

No. He was too close. She would not be allowed to stop him; the goal was in sight. Within two years more he would control all crime of worth in the world. The politicians would be bought, governments overturned or crushed, then he would emerge into the light, in control. Peace would reign... Stephan Krebs sank, exhausted, into a chair and allowed the dream to lull him to sleep.

A signal from his phone awakened him several hours later. A text from Marco. He had landed in America. Rubbing the sleep from his eyes, Stephan thumbed off the phone then made his way to the bedroom for a shower and some clean clothes.

Refreshed from the shower, he realized he was hungry, so headed to the kitchen. After a meal he planned to check on the animals, see how their training was coming along. Marco was on site, there should be some good news within hours. Smiling, Stephan began to prepare an omelette.

MARCO WASN'T HAPPY and he struggled to keep that from showing. He really wanted to strangle the woman at the reception desk, but instead politely asked her to check again.

"Sir, I'm quite sure that no one like you described is here, but I'll check again if it'll make you happy."

"Thank you. I am desperate to find my sister."

The man exuded danger and the girl highly doubted he had a sister. "Sir, I have nothing here. The last patient brought in from Europe was six months ago. Could that have been her?"

"No. I spoke with her just a few days ago. It would have been recent, a week, no more."

"Sorry, can't help you there."

Marco fought to remain calm, but no sign of his inner impatience showed on his face. "Is there a way you can check with other facilities in the country? She may have been taken to another hospital."

"I can contact them and ask, but it could take hours before I get a reply, maybe days." She sighed inwardly as he thanked her and turned away. Slowly she withdrew her finger from the panic button under her desktop. That man was one scary individual.

Gina saw him emerge from the hospital and gunned the engine of her car. The cab leaped forward as he lifted his arm to signal. "Where to, buddy?" she asked as he climbed in the back.

"Airport. Swiftly."

"You got it, Pontiac." She grinned as she whipped out into traffic.

He was studying a list he'd taken from his pocket and didn't notice when she turned into the warehouse district. She was pulling into a building before he realized something was wrong. Instantly he had a gun to her head. "I don't know who you are, or what you think you're doing, but you have fucked with the wrong man."

"*Be silent. Obey me. Put the gun away and get out of the car.*"

Marco, shivering with a nameless terror, obeyed her. Inside he was screaming in terror, but outwardly he made no sign. The small woman got out of the car, tossed aside the cabbie's hat then looked him over. "*Follow me.*" Obediently, Marco followed her into the middle of the open space.

He stood still, trying to track her with his eyes as she slowly walked around him, sizing him up. "*Give me your gun.*" he did. She looked it over then tossed it away. "*Have you other weapons?*"

"Yes."

"*Guns?*"

"No."

"Blades?"

"Yes."

"No matter. Are you Marco?"

"Yes."

"Did Stephan Krebs send you to kill a woman who had been burned?"

"Yes."

She smiled at him then took out her phone. *"Do you know where Stephan Krebs is at this moment?"*

"Yes." He fought himself, hated himself for the weakness and the betrayal he knew was coming, but was helpless to refuse her. He didn't understand how this could happen. It terrified him.

Gina dialed her phone. "Tommy here, talk to me."

"Tommy, this is Gina. I have someone here with information for you. I'll put him on." She held up the phone for Marco to speak into. *"Tell me exactly where to find Stephan Krebs right now."*

Fighting himself all the way, he did, and with her prompting, described the land, castle, and its defences. "Got that Tommy?"

"Every bit of it, Miss Gina. Great work. You on your way home now?"

"I have a small errand to deal with then I'll return as quickly as I can. Please inform her Majesty of my success and impending return."

"Yes ma'am, I'll do that right now. Happy travels." The line went dead then she put the phone back in the pocket of her loose jacket.

Tossing aside the jacket she faced Marco wearing a spandex body suit. *"I release you."*

Suddenly freed from the spell Marco snapped his arms down causing a razor sharp knife to drop into each hand. He leaped at her with amazing speed for so large a man, but he missed completely as she easily dodged away. "Good, Marco. I hoped you would want to play. Now let us do the dance of blood."

Marco took a step back, horrified as she shimmered and changed into a nightmare. She was taller now, more heavily muscled. Her face had elongated and long sharp fangs protruded from her upper jaw. "What the fuck are you?" Marco swallowed hard as he spoke, constantly turning to face her as she paced around him.

"Something very different from you, Marco. Ah well, perhaps not so different at that. We are both predators, you and I, are we not? Now, shall we see who is the stronger predator?" She darted at him.

With a scream of fear and challenge, he counter attacked, the deadly blades flashing. He felt the sting of torn flesh as she passed him. Once again she was pacing, moving around him. There was a small cut on her right arm, but it barely bled. She raised her arm and licked the wound. The bleeding stopped.

"Very good, Marco. It's been centuries since anyone has managed to cut me with a blade."

She continued to pace, and he turned to face her, slowly bleeding from a gash on his chest. The vampire darted in again. His blades flashed and Marco felt the shock of a blade cutting deep even as he felt the pain of her claws. She was gone again, facing him, a smile on her feline features as she showed him the blades she'd ripped from his hands, and tossed them aside. The creature licked her fingers then caressed the wound on her chest; it sealed, and the bleeding stopped.

"What are you," he asked again, the fear in his voice mixed with grudging admiration.

Her voice dropped low, soft and seductive as she stepped closer. "Vampire." She leaped in and he fought with kicks and hammer blows. She blocked his efforts and delivered a few blows of her own. He began to tire, his blows to weaken, then a spinning kick sent him sprawling to the floor.

Marco groaned with pain and tried to strike her, but she was astride his chest now. She caught his wrist and forced it to the floor, the other as well. He tried to head butt her as her fangs slowly descended to his throat.

"You've been more fun than you know, Marco. Be a good boy now and let Momma taste her reward." Her fangs bit deep and he half screamed, half gasped in pain, then slowly went limp. Gina drank greedily for a while, then forced herself to stop. She swung her leg back across him and stood up, delicately dabbing at her lips as she shimmered back into the woman.

"Go ahead," he groaned. "Finish me. Get it over with."

"Oh no, Marco. I'm not going to kill you. You've been far too much fun. Sadly, I do have to make you forget me."

"Believe me, woman," he groaned as he tried to rise and failed, falling loosely onto his back once again, "I could never forget the likes of you."

"*Obey me!*" Once again he shuddered under that commanding spell. "*You have no memory. You do not know who you are, where you came from, or what has happened to you. You will seek out a religious mission and spend the rest of your life helping the poor.*"

Marco lay still, wondering who the woman was. He was still wondering as she got in the cab and drove away.

Once outside Gina stopped the car and let the cabbie out of the trunk. He later found himself sitting in his cab at the airport, a wad of cash in his hand and no memory of where he had been most of the day.

A Fresh Trail

The pacing behind her was driving Kylie crazy. She didn't even look up as she spoke. "Whoever is looking over my shoulder; go have a drink, watch some TV, or go eat somebody, and leave me the hell alone to work."

"Perhaps I should," replied a dangerous voice behind her. Kylie spun around to see the king looming over her.

"Oh crap," she gulped. "Sorry, Sire. American, no monarchy manners and all that. I..."

Ella was already on her feet, but there was no need. Harald laid his hand gently on the girl's shoulders. "No, Kylie, I'm the one who should apologize. We've been caged up here for days and I'm chafing at the delay. Relax, Mother, I'm not going to bite the girl."

"Saw me did you?" Ella chuckled and resumed her seat.

"I did. Perhaps I'll go outside and call Sally while Kylie works."

As Harald stepped outside Kylie worked furiously, muttering to herself. This constant forced togetherness with no action was soon going to send all the vampires into a murderous fit if she couldn't... "There, got you, you bastard."

She sat back and sighed with satisfaction. Harald was smiling as he returned. "I have interesting news."

"You first," grinned Kylie.

"Kylie, you've found him? Talk to me, woman."

"I don't have his location, Sire, but the bastard has gone to ground in England."

"Are you certain? How can you be sure?"

"Sire, he's been hopping around Europe for days. He lands in a country, picks up a rental car, goes to the nearest luxury hotel and settles in, then books a later flight to somewhere else. This time he landed at Heathrow and vanished, no rental car, no hotel booking..." Her computer beeped a signal and she turned. "There, he's booked into a B&B in Derby. He's headed north, but taking a zig-zag, course."

Harald spun to the people at the table. "Eric, can you get us to Edinburgh?" If he's headed north he may be going to Scotland. He needs to keep his captives out of sight. There's plenty of lonely places in the highlands of Scotland."

Eric was already on the phone, making arrangements to have the plane readied. "Harald, what was your news?" asked Ella. "You seemed quite pleased after talking to Sally."

He settled into a chair, the grin returning to his face. "Ah yes, my news. Well, it seems there was some conflict at home. Many of the wolf people struggling to learn both English and the use of technology all at once. The strain was getting to them, and their constant questions about the pups was getting to her, so Sally put Tommy in charge."

Kylie arched an eyebrow at that. "Tommy? Not Amanda or Clyde, or even Peter?"

"Yes. She explained that, due to the time pressure, she needed someone with exceptional organizational skills."

"Oh yeah, that would be Tommy," grinned Terry.

"Well, Tommy seems to have them organized, Olla and Georg are working as teacher's aides to speed up the process and put the shapeshifters at their ease. Gina is intercepting Marco, and my queen has been told to act like one."

"What?"

"Sally wanted to help, but Tommy told her to just stand back and act regal, look disapproving at the pace of developments, and urge them all on to greater efforts. She says he's giving her mad queen lessons. Oh, and it seems that he's chosen a mate."

"What???" That was a chorus of voices.

"Yes. It seems that our shy Tommy has seduced Olla and claimed her. That caused quite a ruckus for a while as the alpha of her pack didn't approve. Sally pulled rank and settled the matter. I'm actually quite proud of my dear Sally."

"You may be proud of Sally," said Kylie, "but I always knew she was made of the right stuff. It's Tommy I'm surprised at. I've never known him to look at a woman, or a man, since I've known him."

Terry grinned and leaned his elbows on the table. "Think about it, Kylie. This is Tommy we're talking about. He never let himself get interested before because of all the secrecy we work under. He wouldn't trust himself not to slip. Olla, now she's another story. She's fully in the know, yet she too needs to keep the shared secrets. She's the perfect choice, from Tommy's perspective."

"Wolves mate for life, Terry," mused Ella. "I hope..."

"Oh, Tommy would have been well aware of all the issues before he made a move, Ella. You know that."

Just then Eric returned with the bus. "Pack up folks, we're ready to go."

They swiftly gathered their things and mounted the bus. During the long drive out of the city to the hangar where the plane was waiting, Kylie phoned the home base in America. "Tommy here, talk to me."

"Tommy, you hound. What's this I hear about you seducing the girls?"

"It's only one girl," came Olla's voice, "and it will remain so. It was I who did the seducing."

Kylie was laughing with delight. "Olla, you she-beast. My poor Tommy, what has she done to you."

"Kylie, you have no idea. She sheds all over... ow."

Tommy was laughing and so was everyone else in the bus. "You sound happy, Tommy. We're all pleased for you both."

"I am happy, Kylie, we both are."

"Kylie, is King Harald with you?"

"I'm here, Olla. What is it?"

"You are the alpha of Tommy's pack. Will you allow this? Will you accept me?"

"Yes to both questions, Olla. Olla, we believe we're closing in on our quarry. I will ask Eric to return for you and Georg once we're certain. Bring a few of your strongest people with you. It will soon be time to reclaim your children."

"I will speak with them right now. Thank you."

Kylie shut off the phone and gave Harald a puzzled look. Gudrun smiled her delight. "Our king is offering our allies some payback, Kylie. He's also reassuring them that he sees them as allies of equal standing and not as inferiors. Am I right, Harald?"

"Spot on, Gudrun. I would much prefer to have the werewolves as allies, but not so much as vassals. I do, however like the idea of having one or two of them as part of our inner circle. The wolf has instincts and abilities that we don't. With their attributes added to our own we'll be much stronger. Plus, we can learn much from them."

"Are you certain, Harald?"

"Think about it, Ella. Wolves are pack animals; loyal to the death. They'll have no trouble fitting in, shifting their allegiance to us. They, along with Peter, who is their friend, can keep the lines of communication open and flowing freely between wolf and vampire."

"You feel this is important?"

"Yes, Mother, I do. The days of us just vanishing into the forest are gone. Worse yet, the humans have such a vast population, and are so fearful. If they discover the existence of..."

"Non-humans?" suggested Terry.

"Exactly. You know as well as I what the consequences of that might be."

Ella pondered for a few moments then reached to gently squeeze his shoulder. "Harald, if we went all this time and were as unaware of the wolf people as the humans were of us, is it possible that still other species are out there?"

"That had crossed my mind," he sighed. "We may have to do some investigating of our own. First, however, we need to eliminate this Stephan Krebs and everyone who has been made aware of the werewolves."

Just then the bus arrived at the hidden hangar. They boarded the plane and headed for Scotland. Once out over the ocean Eric began to swear in Danish. "What is it, Eric?"

"Sorry, Sire," came Eric's voice. "I forgot you could hear me. I'm swinging up north towards Norway. There's a military exercise of British planes right in our path. I thought it best to avoid them."

"A wise decision, Eric," chuckled Harald. "Tell me, is this plane armed?"

"Of course it is," sighed Gudrun. "However, it's no match for several British warplanes. Eric, approach Scotland from the north."

"Yes, ma'am."

"I hear the laughter in your voice, Eric. Don't make me come up there."

"Elsa, please, I'm trying to fly the plane and avoid detection."

Gudrun smiled and glanced at Terry. His face was passive, but his eyes were hard as flint. "Don't be jealous, Terry."

"What??? Sorry, Gudrun, what did I miss?"

"All the fun, Mr. Serious. What is going on in that head of yours?"

"Sorry, old habits."

"Talk to me, handsome. What's going on?"

"It may sound silly, but I'm rehearsing, in my mind."

"Rehearsing what?"

"The coming battle with Krebs. We're closing in, and I want to be ready. This is something I learned from my father. It's helped me capture a number of extremely dangerous people; it kept me alive during the first encounter with Mobutu."

To his surprise she cuddled closer, snuggling down onto his shoulder. "Terry, honey, promise me something," she whispered in his ear.

"Anything, gorgeous," he grinned in reply.

She kissed his cheek and smiled. "I'm being serious now. I've been a mercenary soldier for a long time, Terry. I have the strength and skills to deal with Stephan, and I will. This one is personal for both of us, but I have a prior claim. Promise me, unless there's no other option, the kill is mine."

He sighed deeply then let his shoulders relax. "Can I rough him up first?"

"All right," she laughed, "but only if you're good."

Eric came over the speaker once again. "Coast of Scotland coming up, people. We have no safe houses here nor do we have a landing site. I recommend standard incursion protocols."

Gudrun sat up straight, all business now. "Standard protocols. Yes. Choose a spot and I'll brief the others." She turned to the rest of the passengers. "Standard incursion protocols is for a mission to a location where we have no safety nets in place. Eric will set us down near, but out of sight from, a small community. We'll disguise the plane, Eric will find us transportation, then we can resupply or investigate as needed. Someone will have to remain with the plane to make certain it's safe to return to."

"That will be me," said Ella. "Kylie will want to stay on her computer and work. I can deal with any curious locals."

"Where are we Eric?" asked Gudrun.

"Just about to set down, Gudrun. We're a bit out of Aberdeen. We can gather more information there. We need to stock food, but for now we have plenty of fuel."

"I have contacts in Aberdeen," said Harald. "Just get me into town and I can deal with the rest."

They felt a soft bump then the engines wound down. "Bird has landed," grinned Eric. "Storage hatch is unlocked." He lowered the boarding stairs and sped down; Gudrun close on his heels. The rest watched in admiration as the two mercenaries set to work.

The plane had settled down in a clearing, surrounded by a grove of pine trees. They hauled a huge tarp from the storage compartment and unfolded it. Lines were tossed across the plane and the tarp drawn over to hide it from sight. The camouflage was in place in short order and the plane would be completely invisible from prying eyes on the ground or above. Ella would deal with anyone who got too close.

The tarp was no sooner in place than Eric sped away through the trees. Gudrun turned to the others. "All right, people. Let's just wait until we hear from Eric. Harald, we'll need food and clothing. I doubt you can acquire military gear, but hiking clothes, portable shelters, and food for our human allies would be helpful. We'll need the clothing, but we can hunt for ourselves. I expect you plan to locate Stephan, have Eric drop us off to scope out the situation while he returns for the werewolves."

"You assume correctly, Gudrun. That's exactly what I want to do."

A horn sounded close by. "That'll be Eric," she grinned. "Come."

As they emerged from the trees they saw Eric behind the wheel of an aging land rover. They wedged themselves inside and he started away. "Gudrun, you might want to put a forget spell on that farmer when we return this heap. He was a bit too curious for my liking."

"What, you didn't leave him bound and gagged for somebody else to find? Is he still alive?"

"No, he's alive and counting his money right now. I know I broke protocol there, but Scotland's a friendly, and I believe the rule against killing innocents unnecessarily is still in place."

"It is, my friend," she smiled. "Thank you. I'm sorry, Harald, I know how important this is, but..."

"No, Eric acted wisely. A man counting his money is one thing, the authorities finding a dead body is quite another. I'll use the compulsion on the farmer when we return."

They were on the road for nearly an hour before they reached the city of Aberdeen. Eric and Gudrun set out to gather what supplies they needed while Harald checked in with his contacts. Terry disappeared into the streets. As long as he didn't speak he blended in well enough. Once out of sight he made a phone call. A few minutes later he got a return call. Terry hailed a cab.

The pub had a warm friendly feel to it. Terry bought a pint and chatted with the barman for a bit then retreated to a booth in the corner. Shortly, a tall man in a business suit came in, bought a pint then asked about a Yank. The barman pointed out Terry and the tall man sauntered over to join him.

"Sawchuk, I heard you'd retired, become a private snooper, as it were. I don't think I've ever seen you out of a suit before."

"So take a picture. This is the new uniform."

"Tell me, why should I share information with you, now that you're no longer sanctioned."

"Ever heard of a man called Stephan Krebs?"

"Shh, keep your voice down. Yes, I've heard of him. Why do you ask?"

"I'm tracking him. I think he might be headed this way."

"Sawchuk, you don't want to go there, not with this man. Forget that name. Take a new job. Go fishing for Christ's sake."

"Can't."

"Why not?"

"Because I'm gonna kill the bastard. It's personal. He landed in London yesterday. Today he was in Derby. He's headed north somewhere. I need to know where."

"It's pronounced Darby, and I'll put a few feelers out, but, mark me; this is a mistake."

"Won't be my first," growled Terry as he spotted the barman talking on the phone. The man quickly looked away, but it was too late. "Aw fuck."

"What?"

"The bartender. Why does everybody always look right at the person they're talking about. I'd bet a month's pay Krebs is on to me now."

"Then run, hide," replied his companion. He drained his glass then rose from the table and walked away.

Terry drained his glass then he too rose to leave. "Great beer," he said cheerily. "Nice and rich, a full meal in a glass."

He waved at the barman then stepped out into the sunshine. A huge man bumped into him as soon as he was through the door. "Watch where you're going, bloody wanker," growled the big man. He reached to push Terry against the stone wall, but the shorter man moved first.

Terry's fist sank deeply into the big man's solar plexus, driving the air from his lungs with a loud whoosh. As the man doubled over Terry caught him and kicked the back of his knee then lowered him gently to the ground. "Easy, easy. Short breaths, short breaths. That's it, you're getting some air in now. Breathe deeper, that's it. Now, here's a piece of advice from me to you. Never talk when you should be doing. It relaxes your abs leaving you open to that punch."

The big man groaned and shifted his weight, groping at his pocket. "Looking for this?" asked Terry as he held up the man's switchblade knife. "This is a real beauty; I think I'll keep it. You try anything stupid and I'll put it through your kidneys, understand?"

"Aye, I understand, Yank."

"Good. It's been fun chatting with you and all, but, I have somewhere else to be. If you're smart you won't try to follow." He rose and stepped away from the big man, raising his hand to hail a taxi.

Terry arrived back at the old Land Rover to find it loaded and everybody waiting for him. "Where were you?" asked Gudrun, who was in Elsa form.

"You know where I was," he replied, as he moved to climb into the vehicle.

She caught his arm and spun him around, going nose to nose with him. "I know roughly where you were, and I know you were in a fight. However, I don't know exactly where you were, what you were doing, or who you were fighting with. I also have no idea why you're so angry."

He turned away from her and heaved himself inside the car. She got in tight to his side. "All right, I'm pissed off because that bastard Krebs is on to me, probably has been for a while. I beat up one of the local thugs because he was supposed to rough me up and he was available."

"A little more detail please," she said softly as Eric pulled out into traffic.

"I made contact with a British agent I know. I was lucky. He was in this city and agreed to meet me. As soon as I mentioned Krebs he told me to back off and ran away. As soon as the big-eared bartender heard Krebs' name he was on the phone. I stepped out of the bar and Krebs' man was waiting."

"And you fought him alone?"

"We fought, we talked, he gave me a present for you." Terry handed her the switchblade.

"Pretty. So, am I being told to stop mothering you, that you can handle yourself?"

"No, not really," he sighed. "I kinda like it."

Harald chuckled at that. "Tell me, Terry, what makes you so certain Krebs is on to us?"

"He's been on to us all along, Sire. Every time he landed he used a credit card to rent a car. When he finally landed where his own car was located he used that same credit card to rent a room and buy fuel. He's leaving me a trail. I suspect one of my old contacts tipped him off back in Denmark. He probably thinks I'm alone and wants to get me well out of the cities where he can take me down and lose the body."

"Son of a bitch."

"Yes, Sire," muttered Eric, "that he is."

They dropped off their supplies, then Harald went with Eric to put the compulsion on the farmer. By the time they all got back to the plane, Kylie was outside throwing rocks at trees and swearing profusely. Ella was watching, an amused smile on her face.

"So, you figured out the credit card, did you Kylie?"

"Yeah, I did, Terry. I should have seen it sooner."

"It doesn't matter," said Ella. "Even if he knows we hunt him, he's still leading us to his whereabouts. Is that not what we wanted?"

"Yes it..." Harald stopped speaking as Kylie held up her hand and snatched at her phone.

"Tommy, tell me good news."

"Miss Gina was successful. Incoming message." Another man's voice, devoid of all emotion came on, giving detailed directions to Stephan Krebs' hideout.

"Tell Gina I said well done," said Harald, who had stepped closer. "All right. Eric, can you find this place from the air without being detected?"

"I can."

"The we're in business. I want to spend a bit of time studying the lay of the land. Drop us nearby then head back to the U.S.A. and collect the shapeshifters. We'll plot and plan while you're gone."

The camouflage was swiftly withdrawn, stored in the plane, and they were back in the air. Harald had gone sombre, withdrawn. Ella had seen this before, many times. King Harald the Saxon was about to lead his people into battle against a much larger foe, one who knew he was coming. It certainly wasn't the first time, but it was the first in centuries.

STEPHAN KREBS NODDED his approval as he watched the wolf pups attack the man in the padded training suit. They bitterly resented being treated like dogs, but that what's they were, animals. They would be trained as such. They had to learn their place. They were learning and growing fast. He kept them in animal form, fed them dog food, and only allowed human form at the end of day for a short time.

Stephan spoke softly to the man in the expensive suit who was constantly at his right hand. "It's going well; bring them here for a moment." The man raised his arm and whistled. The young wolves came, nearly two dozen in all. "Assume human form," he commanded them.

They shimmered into naked children of various ages, all wearing electronic collars. Stephan addressed them in the broken Russian they knew. The younger ones were having trouble grasping English.

"You're doing well, my pretty dogs; I'm pleased with you. Soon you will have an opportunity to test yourselves against a living human target. When the fool arrives here, you will hunt him as a pack, find him, and kill him. Do you understand?"

"Da, we understand," replied one of the oldest.

"Good." Stephan gave him that icy smile he'd worn the day he captured them. "Do this well. Please me in this and you'll earn a reward. An additional two hours each day in human form for a whole month. Now, back to your training."

He watched impassively as they shimmered back into wolf form and returned to the training area. "I'm well pleased with this location, however, as soon as this current adventure is complete we'll return to Finland. Now, I have another task for you."

"Sir?"

"Marco hasn't checked in yet. I don't like this; he's never late. Also, he's not answering his phone."

"Could he have been apprehended by the American authorities?"

"No, had that been so, my people would have known and freed him instantly. No, something else is amiss. It could be no more than still trying to track the bitch down and his phone run out of charge, but I must know. Contact our people in America, see if they can locate him."

"Yes, sir." The man stepped away a short distance so his voice wouldn't disturb his boss who was now studying the defensive systems.

"Also, call in another two dozen troops."

"Sir?"

"At once."

"Yes, sir."

Stephan tried to focus, but he couldn't get that woman's face out of his mind. "Dammit, Ariel, or Gudrun, or whoever the hell you are. It isn't possible you could have defeated Marco, is it? No, that's not possible. Those damned paranoid Americans have detained him for some reason. If I don't hear from him today I'll have to pull some very tight strings to find him."

His musings were interrupted by the buzzing of his phone. Irritably, he jerked it from the pocket of his jacket and thumbed it open. There was a picture of several people gathered by an old Land Rover. He recognized one of the men.

"Eric, so, by some deep misfortune you're still alive. So it's you who tracks me, is it? Well then, this will be more fun than I originally imagined. I'll be sure to tell you how I enjoyed listening to her scream as the fire engulfed her. Then I'll kill you personally.

"Only two men and a woman? Truly? You should have come with more than that." In spite of himself, and his bravado, Stephan Krebs shivered.

Eric was no fool, and he was a deadly soldier. If his companions were of the same calibre, this could go badly. That group was about the usual size for one of Ariel's surgical strikes. They would find him. They would come swiftly, silently, and strike hard. Stephan was suddenly very glad he'd asked for more men. Now he just hoped they would arrive first.

For the rest of the day he fussed and fretted. It had been years since anyone managed to unsettle him like this. He didn't like it, not at all, and everywhere he looked he saw her face, mocking him. As he paced about the old castle, the wolves slunk away from him, and his men found things to do to keep busy, never making eye contact. No one wanted to give him an outlet for his temper.

It was nearly dark when he returned to the apartments and made himself a meal. He was about to enjoy the first bite when the man in the suit came hurrying in. "What is it? Well, speak up."

"Sir, it's Marco. They found him."

"And?"

"He's in a street mission, helping to serve the homeless in the soup kitchen."

"What???"

"Sir, they say he has no memory, doesn't know who he is, not even his name. They say he's weak, and trembles as he moves, like a man who has lost a lot of blood, or taken too many drugs."

"Are they certain it's Marco?"

Silently the man passed over his phone with a picture on it. With a howl of rage and loss, Stephan hurled the phone across the room. The man retrieved it and slipped out, closing the door and leaving his boss alone with his meal. The meal remained on the plate, growing cold. Stephan Krebs had lost his appetite.

He was still pacing about the room hours later when all the alarms were triggered through out the castle grounds. Flood lights sprang to life, turning the grounds from night to bright daytime. Stephan came running out, gun in hand, to find armed men searching everywhere. "What is it? What's happened?"

"Unknown, sir," replied one of his soldiers. "Something tripped the alarms, but..."

"But what? What was it?"

"Sir, here's what the camera caught," replied the man, turning the monitor at his side so Stephan could see it.

"That...that's impossible. What kind of a joke is this?"

"It's not a joke, Sir," the man replied evenly. "That's what triggered the alarms. The man on the outer watch station is dead, torn apart."

Stephan Krebs didn't reply. His mind raced wildly in fear, a fear that he dared not allow to show on his face. What he saw on the monitor was a sabre-toothed tiger carrying one of the wolf pups in its jaws.

LITTLE NIKKA LAY STILL in the jaws of the tigress as she was carried along, down to the sea, through the waters and up into the hills. She heard others close by but couldn't see them. Eventually she almost fell asleep. She remembered being carried this way by her mother long ago. Nikka fully expected to be eaten, but the tiger was surprisingly gentle; it was almost comforting.

Finally the beast dropped her and she looked into those cold glowing eyes. Nikka braced herself for death, but instead the tigress shimmered into a woman. It took a moment to understand, then she too shimmered into human form. The strange woman took hold of Nikka's collar with both hands and snapped the lock that held it in place. She passed it to a big man who ground it under his boot, silencing the constant beeping noise it had made.

"What is your name, child?" The big man spoke to her, but she didn't understand him. "Try in Russian, Mother."

The strange woman was pulling on clothes a dark woman had given her. She spoke in Russian. "I understand," she replied. "My name is Nikka." She shivered in the cold air and the dark woman wrapped her in a blanket then lifted her up in her arms. Nikka buried her face in the woman's neck and began to sob uncontrollably as she clung on tightly.

Kylie continued to coo soothing sounds and to hold the girl gently. "Ella honey, tell her she's safe now. Tell her we won't let the bad man hurt her anymore." Ella nodded and spoke gently to the child. It took a few tries then the girl started to settle down, but she continued to cling to Kylie.

The big man began to question her through the tiger woman. "Nikka, how many more wolf children are there in the compound?"

She thought for a moment until she understood what was wanted then began to count on her fingers. The answer was twenty-three. "Are they all wearing collars like that one?"

"Yes, sir. All Master's dogs have to wear the collars. If we don't do well the collars choke us."

The tiger woman reached out to gently caress the girl's cheek, brushing away the last of the tears. "You're not a dog, my child," she said gently. "You're a wolf. No one has a right to put such a collar on you. He will pay for that insult."

"Are you the Great Mother? The one Peter told our people about?"

"Yes."

"Are you going to kill the master?"

"Yes, we are. We'll kill him and bright back your friends."

"Can you bring my father back? Master killed him the day he captured us."

"No, I'm sorry, child. That I cannot do."

Saddened, the child snuggled deeper into Kylie's arms. Kylie carried her to a sleeping bag and tucked her in then lay down beside her and sang a soft lullaby. Nikka snuggled close and was soon asleep.

Terry silently ghosted back into their small camp in the trees. "All clear. No pursuit."

"Very good," replied Harald as he sank to the ground beside the fire. The others joined him. "All right, people, what did we learn?"

"Their perimeter is completely dependant on electronics," said Gudrun. "I located the command centre but didn't disable it. I'll save that for the incursion. They also have men on watch carrying automatic weapons."

Harald nodded. "Mother?"

"I killed one of the watchmen, then deliberately set off the alarms as I captured the child. I expect Krebs is now staring at a photo of a sabre-toothed tiger with a wolf cub in its jaws."

"That should rattle his nerves a bit," chuckled Terry. "Do you think it was wise to allow the photo?"

"Who would believe it wasn't faked?" grinned Ella. Terry matched her grin and nodded.

"What did you see from the hillside, Sire?" asked Gudrun.

"I'm sure you noticed as well, Gudrun. They're vulnerable from the windward side of the island. The children are housed close to the wall there, but the men are billeted farther away, closer to the trees. They're depending on that wall for protection, that's their weak point."

He began sketching in the dirt beside the fire. "We'll deploy the wolves here, in the forest. They'll wait for our signal then attack. The Vampires will scale the wall, then attack from within. That'll be the signal to the shapeshifters.

"Gudrun, your task is to disable the electronic defences. Once they're down, find Krebs and kill him. Take no chances, but get it done. Ella, your task is to release and defend the children. Take Nikka with you so she can reassure them it is safe." Ella nodded her agreement.

"Terry, you've proved stronger and more resourceful than I ever expected. I'll ask you to lead the wolves to their stations then lead them into the fray. Once they're inside, you join Gudrun in her hunt."

"What of Eric, Vassily, and Jimmy?"

Harald chuckled. "I'd like to borrow your soldiers if I may, Gudrun, since I'm going to be the most obvious target for the gunmen."

"You're a wise man, my king," laughed Gudrun.

Just then Harald's phone rang. He listened for a moment then thumbed it off. "We must lay low for a while. Eric is confined by weather for a few hours, so he says. He's bringing all the vampires, five wolves, Jimmy, and Vassily."

Everyone was settling down when Harald noticed Gudrun was missing. He nodded his approval. The rest of the night passed quietly. The sun was well up, yet the young wolf was the only one awake as Gudrun returned to the camp. She had shifted back to her natural appearance. "Shh, it's only me," she whispered in Russian.

"Gudrun," rumbled Harald's voice, "who's on watch?"

"Terry's on lookout. He says he has a bad feeling about this. He says, and I agree, we should be watching for an escape route by sea."

Harald rolled easily to his feet. "I had thought of that possibility. Since we're stuck here for another day, perhaps you and I should see what we can find once darkness comes."

Ella rose gracefully to her feet and smiled. "No, you two go hunting. You need to be well fed for the battle. When darkness falls the cat will go exploring. If there is a sea route out of there I'll find and disable it."

Harald nodded his agreement just as Terry ghosted back into the camp. "Things just got worse," he growled as he sank to the ground. "Kylie, you got anything us mere mortals can eat?" Laughing, she tossed him two energy bars.

"What has happened, Terry?" asked Harald.

"Krebs just got in a truck load of reinforcements, Sire. They're not military, but they are heavily armed. I suspect they're mob soldiers."

"Dangerous, but undisciplined," nodded Harald. "It looks like I have my work cut out for me."

"Harald..."

"Relax, Mother. Remember Sothcar's Ridge against the Vikings? We were in worse shape then, but we managed a victory."

"Those were the days of swords and spears, Harald," she reminded him. "Guns are far more deadly and efficient. We're facing plenty of those."

"I understand," he sighed, sobering. "Gudrun, advise me. How do we counter the guns?"

She knelt and scooped the dirt with her hands, making a swift mock up of the castle. "Here, Sire, where we plan to scale the wall. I suggest we leave Vassily and Jimmy on the top of the wall. They'll have night scopes and can act as snipers. They're exceptionally good at this and will be able to minimize the effect of the weapons you face. We can easily deploy Eric here behind this portion of fallen wall with great effect.

"You, Peter, and Gina cause a fuss right here drawing the attention away from the electronics centre. I'll disable it then join you."

"No, disable the defences then begin your hunt."

"I'd rather wait for Terry," she grinned. "I promised he could rough Krebs up before I kill him."

"It works for me," grinned the king. "So, now we watch and wait until our people arrive."

Kylie sighed deeply then started to finger comb Nikka's hair. "I'm feeling a bit like a third wheel here. I can handle myself in a fight, people."

"Kylie..."

"No Ella, you're not allowed to keep me in a glass cage. If this was a team mission in the old days I'd be in the thick of it."

"Actually, Kylie, I have another important task for you."

"Sire?"

"Are you any good as a sniper?"

"I'm a fair shot, why?"

"No one must escape this, Kylie, you know that. Those people down there are going to see us, and they'll know. They must not be allowed to escape. I need a sniper on that hill overlooking the drawbridge. Have you ever killed a man?"

Kylie dropped her gaze. "No."

"Can you? Don't hold back. If there's any doubt, even the slightest chance you might hesitate, say so. I can assign another to that position."

"No, I can do it."

"Kylie?"

"I can, Ella. I know what's at stake here; I know what you guys are risking to help these people. I'll do it, Harald. I won't fail you."

"Accepted. All right, we have a plan. Gudrun, all this is assuming there'll be weapons on that plane."

"This is Eric we're talking about. There'll be weapons, and body armour. There'll also be at least one rocket launcher with heat seeking ordinance. Kylie should have that with her in case a vehicle makes a run for it."

"Eric. That man is a wonder," mused Harald. "Gudrun, when all this is finished, I want you and Eric to develop a training regime for us all. Weapons and modern combat strategies. I have a lot of catching up to do."

They spent the rest of the day keeping watch, but nothing else came or went from the small island. Men could be seen searching the trees and shoreline, all to no avail. Through the field glasses they watched as the men replaced the outer watch station with trip wires and booby traps.

Terry made notes of the work and the locations of the traps. He knew he couldn't be aware of them all, but he would have an idea of their pattern.

STEPHAN KREBS WAS INDEED rattled, but he was a long way from finished. Without Marco as his aide, he took full charge himself. Supervising the layout of the booby traps, the building of temporary cover for his soldiers kept his mind busy. He cursed himself for not having a squad of mercenaries stationed with him at all times.

Stephan had become too dependant on Marco. He'd thought the man invincible, but, somehow, someone had taken him down. In this modern world, technology could bring down the strongest of men. He knew that all too well, and now Marco was gone. Stephan felt an emptiness inside him at the loss of Marco. He couldn't name it, and he didn't like it. It made him feel weak.

A sudden flash of light from the hillside overlooking the island caught his eyes. It was there for just a heartbeat then it was gone. "I know you're there, Eric. I know it's you who's had that damned American on my trail. I know you'll come in the night. Come then; I'll be waiting. We will finish that old contest, although it no longer matters. The woman is ruined forever even if she does manage to survive. Neither of us will have her. Come to me, Eric. Come and meet your fate."

He strode purposefully to the dog pens. "Human form," he barked, and they shimmered into the half starved children. "Listen carefully. Tonight, men will come. They will attack from the trees. The men with guns will not be able to stop them all, some will reach the inner compound.

"Once they're inside the walls it will be your task to kill them. You will fight in wolf form, sink your fangs into the enemy, rend the flesh from their bones then feed on your kill. Tonight will be your night, do you understand?"

"Da, we understand," replied the eldest, a boy of about fifteen.

"Good, now resume dog form and rest. There'll be no training today." With that he turned and strode away, not even bothering to watch or make certain they obeyed him.

"Tonight is the night we kill you," muttered the boy before he and the others shimmered back to wolf form.

Stephan retreated to his rooms and ate a meagre meal. That didn't seem to help so he poured a generous glass of cognac. "Rest, I need to rest." He did try but couldn't stop pacing about. Her face continued to haunt him as he slowly slipped into madness. A madness driven by fear.

The day was well on, near sunset, before he decided to check all the monitors again. Every instinct he had was screaming at him to flee. What could be wrong now, was Eric actually going to attack before full darkness? He stopped before the main monitor and began flicking from camera to camera. All was quiet.

With a sudden feeling of dread, he switched the screen to the dock and the boat hidden in the shallow sea cave.

That escape route had been one of the big drawing cards for Stephan when he bought this place. A final bolt hole in case of disaster. The screen showed everything to be normal, then he saw the movement. It was the goddamned sabre-toothed tiger. Somehow it had loosened the moorings. It was poking at the boat, moving it out further into the waters. "Nooo!!!"

He snatched up an automatic weapon and raced to the dog pens. "You, with me," he said as he pointed to the largest wolf then raced away. The wolf was right at his heels. He fought the lock on the old door then yanked it open, racing down the tunnel to the cave below. Arriving at the dock he saw the boat, now well out of his reach, drifting away with the tiger swimming behind it.

Stephan emptied his gun at the beast, but she had dived below the surface, and he missed. "Kill that damned thing," he ordered, waving his arm in the general direction of the boat. Kill!"

Obediently, the young wolf leaped into the sea and swam after the retreating form of the tigress. As he reached her his jaws opened, but she was far too fast and strong for him. She grabbed him in powerful jaws and dragged him below the surface. With a howl of frustration and blind rage, Stephan hurled the gun after the boat which was now in the grasp of the ebbing tide. His escape plan was ruined, the boat gone forever. Only the hidden jet ski remained, and he could carry nothing with him if he had to use it.

The young wolf fought desperately with fang and claw, terrified below the surface of the water. He was unaware as the tiger shimmered into a woman. She ignored his fangs and claws that raked across her skin as she grabbed the collar and tore it off him. She then seized him by the scruff and pulled him back to the surface, keeping the boat between her and Krebs line of sight.

"Breathe, breathe," she commanded softly in Russian. Choking and coughing, he managed to shimmer into human form. "That's better. Breathe deeply now. All right, we have a long swim ahead of us. Are you able to make it or do you want to ride on the cat's back?"

"I can swim better as wolf. Who are you? Why are you helping me?"

"I'm a friend. Last night I took Nikka to safety. I will now take you to her if you wish."

"She's alive, my sister? We saw you take her. We thought you had eaten her."

"She's alive and safe." Ella smiled. "We must swim beneath the surface. It'll be easier in human form."

"I can't swim well in this form."

"Hold to my shoulders then. When it's safe we'll change back and run to my friends together. What say you, young wolf, will you run with the tiger? Will you trust me?"

"I will. You're the Great Mother the elders tell stories of."

"Yes, that's who I am. Cling to my shoulders now and hold your breath." She rolled easily in the water, and, sucking in as much air as he could manage, he gripped her shoulders tightly.

They surfaced only twice before reaching the rocky shore far from the island of torment. They shimmered into animal form before leaving the water and scrambling up the bank into the trees. Once within the shelter of the trees they shook the water from their coats then set out.

The wolf stayed close behind as the great cat made her way through the forest and up the hills to her camp. Suddenly catching a familiar scent, he raced past her, bounded into the camp, and leaped on Nikka, licking her face and causing her to squeal in protest.

"Igor, stop it, stop." She laughed as he slobbered her face again then shifted into human form and gathered her into his arms.

STEPHAN KREBS STALKED back to the main compound. With a jerk of his head he signalled one man to come to him. "Sir?"

"Take some explosives and bring that cave roof down. Make certain it is completely blocked. I don't want anyone sneaking up on us from behind."

"But, sir, the boat..."

"Is gone. Do as I bid you. Do it now."

"Yes, sir. Right away, sir." Fearfully, the man hurried about the business.

As the man worked, Stephan returned to his apartments and poured a generous glass of cognac. He drank it straight down then poured another. His hands were still trembling.

"That eternally damned sabre-tooth, how the hell is that abomination even here? How in God's name did Eric find and tame the cursed thing? How did it know how to set loose the boat? How did it..." He stopped pacing as the truth hit him.

"Of course, it has to be, it's the only answer. It stands to reason if there are werewolves then there could be werecats. That's the answer. The goddamned thing is a human hybrid. Eric isn't controlling it, he's paying it. Dirty stinking son of a bitch.

"But what if he is controlling it? If he is there is nothing I can do about that except kill it. On the other hand, if he's paying it, then perhaps I can buy its loyalty. No, there's no time. We'll just have to kill it if it's still alive. Perhaps I got lucky and it drowned along with the dog. Pity about the dog, it was my strongest." He took another swallow of the cognac then poured another.

For the rest of the day he paced and fumed, making sure the defenses were in order. As the sun began to set he became more and more agitated. The moon rose, a slender sickle in a deep blue/black sky peppered with glittering, uncaring stars. By the time dawn was approaching with no sign of the enemy, Stephan's nerves were near the breaking point.

Once again he retreated to his rooms to think and compose himself. This wasn't acceptable. He was the man of the iron will. He was the man of ice in the veins. He was the one who never lost control of his emotions. He was the one who broke all others. He would not be broken by a mere soldier, a professional scrounge. He would not allow Eric to destroy him with these games. But the woman's face mocked him.

"So, you want to play psychological games with me, do you Eric? You don't have the skills for it. All you've actually got is a few mercenaries and a trained tiger. Well, I can play this game too. I will relax and await your pleasure."

Even as he spoke to himself aloud to reaffirm his resolve, he heard the voice of Marco in his mind. "They're trying to break you, Stephan. Leave this place then let them drive themselves crazy trying to find you. Pick them off one at a time. You're like a rat in corner here. Get out. Be safe."

Ah, Marco. They had met shortly after Stephan had left Ariel's employ. They had become friends instantly. Marco may not have understood Stephan's mission in life, but he was quite willing to go along with it. "Why world peace?" Marco had asked.

"Because all the greats have tried and failed to accomplish it, Marco. Besides, this war thing is uncontrollable, it gets out of hand too easily. I want full and complete control."

Marco had laughed at that. "Then I will help you achieve it, Stephan." But now Marco was no longer able to help him.

"Alas, my old friend, you're gone, I'm alone here, and now there's no way for me to leave this place. My sanctuary has become my cage. No, I must await Eric's pleasure with this one, but I'll enjoy killing him slowly when he arrives."

With that thought firmly in mind he drifted off to a fitful sleep. He lay fully dressed on the bed, tossing and turning in his sleep as in dreams he fought for his life. In the dream it wasn't Eric he faced, it was Ariel and she had turned into a sabre-toothed tigress.

As Stephan finally succumbed to a troubled sleep, a plane dropped swiftly to the ground many miles away on a hillside. The camouflage tarp was hauled over it and staked in place. Several people shouldered backpacks then set out. They arrived in Harald's camp at noon.

Preparing For Battle

"Igor, Nikka!"

"Grandfather!" Both young ones hurled themselves into Illya's arms. He dropped his pack and knelt to hug them tightly to him. "Grandfather, he said you were dead. Master said you were dead."

"No, child, I am very much alive. Nikka, that terrible man is not your master. I'm alive and have come to kill him. Anna is back in the home of the Great King, Harald, who sent his people to help us. She will be so excited to see you both safe."

"Father?"

"I'm sorry, Nikka. Owan is dead as is Sten. However, before he died Owan managed to convince the Great Mother to help us. It was she who informed the king of what had happened to the people of the wolf."

"Yes, Pappa, it was she who saved us from the master. See, she is there."

"I see her," Illya smiled through his tears.

"May I speak?" asked Olla as she knelt beside them.

"You need no longer ask, Olla. You are of another pack now and owe no respect to me any longer."

"I'll always respect you, Illya. You know this. Igor, are..."

"Only Tikka and Jan remain, Olla," replied the boy. "Ored defied the master and was thrown into the pit with the dogs. He killed three before they finished him. He was my friend and I've sworn to avenge him. I must speak with the king."

Harald was standing slightly apart from the others, expertly spinning a great sword and a long dagger in his hands. The well polished steel blades spun and danced in the air, the sun glittering off them as they flew. "So, Harald, Sally sent you a present." Ella was grinning at him.

"Indeed so. She knows me well. She knows I'll be a lot happier with a blade in my hand."

Peter had heard the boy and his grandfather talking. He caught Harald's attention and the king approached, signalling for the others. When everyone was gathered round, he nodded at the boy who bowed his head and spoke. Peter translated.

"Great king, I must return. The master knows you will attack him. He has ordered all of us to fight and kill you and your people when you reach the compound. I must return and kill him first so that will not happen."

Harald knelt on one knee to be at eye level with the boy. He reached out to put a hand gently on the lad's shoulder, then spoke. Peter translated for them. "Which would you rather do, young warrior, kill Krebs or save your friends?"

The boy swallowed hard then raised his eyes to Harald's. "Save my friends."

Harald gave him a smile of approval, pleased that Krebs hadn't managed to break the boy or destroy his humanity. "When we attack, you will go with Mother to free your friends. Wolf and Vampire will not fight each other this night. We'll fight together as allies. You go with Mother to protect the young ones. Nikka will stay with Kylie, away from the battle." He patted the boy's shoulder then rose.

"Illya, Terry's an experienced agent and has my complete trust. I ask that you give him the same. He'll lead you and the wolves to the forest and then into the battle." Illya nodded and Terry approached to brief his charges.

While Terry spoke, drawing maps on the ground, Igor felt eyes on him. It was the Great Mother. She smiled and patted the ground beside her. He came and sat. "Tonight will be the night," she said in Russian. He nodded. "Are you nervous?"

"Da. I'm afraid as well. Great Mother, every instinct I have says run away. But I can't. I'm the strongest; the others look to me to lead the pack. I must return to free them if I can."

"And you will." She smiled reassuringly at the boy. "Tonight, we hunt together, you and I. We will cross the wall closest to the pens where the young ones sleep. We will remove their collars then keep them close and safe until the fighting is over. This we must do together, yes?"

"Yes," he breathed. To run with and fight beside the Great Mother, to rescue his younger kin and set them free. Dreams beyond dreams. During all the long months of torture, pain, and starvation he had kept himself sane with such dreams. And now they would come true.

The afternoon faded into evening and the drilling went on. Once Terry was satisfied that the wolves would follow his lead, and they fully knew his scent, his group joined the rest. Gudrun continued to drill them on the battle plan. Over and over she demanded they repeat back to her what their mission was, their place in the advance, their main targets, etc. By the time darkness fell she was satisfied each person knew what to do.

She noticed Harald smiling at her, a grim smile of appreciation. He gave her the nod of approval as he rose to signal them to move out. That wasn't the approval of the leader, or of a friend, it was the approval of a battle hardened warrior king. A man who had been extremely successful at war. A fellow soldier, a fellow warrior.

Gudrun was the best in the world at what she did, and she knew it. It was, however, more than gratifying to be recognized for that by the king. Especially this king. In the time since they'd established the monarchy she had come to know this man, and admire him, for his wisdom and leadership abilities as well as admiring him as a person, a king she could serve. This night she planned to prove her worth, that and exact revenge on Stephan Krebs. Gudrun was enjoying herself as they marched along.

The trail they followed wound down the hill and around to a small vale that led down to the sea. They relaxed as they walked, being completely out of sight from the castle. Harald grinned as he caught the slight movement from the top of the hill. Gudrun. If Krebs had managed to send snipers ashore, they would never return.

They reached the end of the small valley. From this point on they would be within sight of the castle. Harald looked up to see Gudrun's signal for them to wait. He softly called a halt. A few moments later she approached, grinning. In her hands was a camera device as well as an explosive. She had disabled both. "I suggest we wait for an hour or so, my king."

"Oh?"

"Yes. There's a thick fog bank rolling in. It will cover our approach and cut down some of the effectiveness of their guns. It's much harder to hit a target you can't see."

INSIDE THE COMPOUND, Stephan Krebs paced and waited. "So, will it be tonight, Eric? Will your patience run out this time? Will you now come meet your fate? I'm waiting for you, my old nemesis. I know it was you. Without you dragging your heels and whispering lies in her ear, Ariel would have come to me. By all the gods, with her at my side I would have already succeeded. The world would already be mine.

"No matter. I will finish you and then begin again. Put the pieces back together and continue. I'll steal your tiger and make good use of her, Eric. Perhaps I'll have her kill you for what you did to Marco.

"Ah, poor Marco. What did you do to him, I wonder. How did you manage to overcome him? Those damned American with their secret drugs. I'll eventually find out what it was and use it against them. I will have my revenge, this I swear.

"Do you hear, Marco. I will avenge you. When this is over I'll send for you. Take you to the best doctors in Europe. If there is any way at all to restore you, old friend, I'll find it. Trust me. I won't leave you like this.

"Do you hear me, Eric, you bastard? I will avenge him. I will cut your heart out and feed it to you." He shouted and raved, but the walls were thick. The men outside could barely hear his roar, and Eric, on the other side of the rising waters, didn't hear him at all.

Pity that. It would have made him smile.

Stephan continued his pacing, but didn't go outside to join his men. For the tenth time he started for the door then stopped. It was a bitter pill to swallow, but he couldn't deny the dark pit in his stomach was fear. He knew Eric, knew him well enough to fear him almost as much as he had feared Ariel.

Deep in his heart, Stephan was a coward, a fearful man. He'd enjoyed being a soldier because he got to use weapons and had others like him to help and shield him. That had been Marco's charm. That was what he had liked so much about Marco. Above all else, Marco had made him feel safe, had a quiet way of allaying his fears. God, how he wished Marco was here now to give him courage.

Stephan poured another glass of cognac and tossed it back, allowing the drink to warm his throat and quiet his fears. After all, Eric might not come this night either. Alas, in his heart he knew, this would be the night. Each moment of delay on Eric's part might see his quarry slip away, gain more support, or the whole mission might be discovered by the authorities. Eric couldn't afford to wait any longer. This night he would come.

Battle Joined

Harald grinned as the fog rolled in and blanketed the area. "Gudrun, I don't think snipers will be of much use this night."

"Indeed not, my king. I'll lead my men in at your side instead."

"So be it. Terry, are you ready?"

"Ready, Sire. I'll give you an hour to get in position then I'll set off one of their booby traps. That should get their attention."

"It will. We'll attack them from behind as soon as you give that signal. Once you hear battle joined, come in from the south. Gudrun will have the alarms and remote triggers disabled by then."

"Right. We're ready," he replied as he scrambled into a wet suit.

"Terry, what is that you keep looking at?" asked Illya.

"It's a compass. See here, this needle always points north. The trees we want to reach are over here at twenty degrees. I've set this to guide me, especially in the fog."

Illya nodded slowly. "Can you not smell the trees, Terry?"

"Nope, I can't."

"How did your species ever rise to dominate the world?" sighed Illya.

"I often ask myself that same question," replied Terry, as he led them into the cold waters of the North Atlantic.

Fortunately, the tide wasn't all the way in, and the water barely reached his chest. The shapeshifters remained in human form, holding weapons high above the water. They moved slowly, feeling their way along the bottom so as not to fall in and cause a splash that might alert the enemy.

They reached the shore and Terry shed his wet suit. He pulled on the military fatigues Eric had provided and slipped on the Kevlar vest. Georg passed him the weapons he'd carried over then all the

132

werewolves shimmered into wolf form. Terry pulled on the night vision goggles and led them into the trees.

The wolves slipped ahead of him, and Terry cursed them silently. He relaxed again as they swiftly found the trail and the first of the traps. He disarmed it, then they sought out the next.

As Terry disarmed the last trap he checked his watch. Two minutes to go. He pulled the flash grenade from the pocket of his fatigues and tapped it to warn the wolves to look away. At the appointed moment he pulled the pin and launched the grenade toward the low pile of stone that had once been part of the castle wall.

As Terry led his team into the water Ella transformed into the cat. The boy shimmered into the wolf, then stepped to her side. The vampires shimmered into the half beasts, all except Gudrun. Still in her battle fatigues and heavily armed with modern weapons, she ghosted on ahead, her soldiers close behind her. The vampires followed, then the wolf and tiger brought up the rear.

Gudrun led them along the shore, then under the drawbridge and up the steep bank on the other side. It was slippery going, but the fog was thick, hiding their passage and muffling any small sound they may have made. When they all reached the base of the wall Gudrun tapped the young wolf on the shoulder. He shimmered back into human form, a questioning look on his face.

She bent low to whisper in his ear. "Can you climb this wall in wolf form?" He shook his head no. "In human form?" Again no. "Then hang on tight." she made eye contact with the tiger then lifted the boy onto the beast's back. He felt the great beast's muscles rippling beneath him as she waited impatiently for the signal.

Suddenly there was a loud bang and a flash of light at the other side of the castle. He almost screamed as the cat launched herself from the ground to land atop the wall then drop down right beside the dog pens. There were a few whimpers from within, but he hissed at them to be quiet. Catching his scent, they all came closer in time to see the cat shimmer into a woman.

Gudrun had leaped beside Ella and easily pulled herself to the top of the wall. Harald grabbed Eric and tossed him up for Gudrun to catch. Jimmy followed and then Vassily. They dropped to the ground inside, weapons at the ready as the vampires easily scaled the wall and joined them.

Gudrun crouched low and moved silently across the courtyard. Her soldiers covering her progress until the fog swallowed her. She reached the electronics control center, smiling with delight to find the door open. She leaped inside and drove a long knife through the body of the one man inside. A few moments later the entire complex was without electronic defences.

She grinned as she ghosted back to the others then shimmered from Elsa into her true human form. "All is ready, my king."

"Well done, Gudrun. Ready, people?"

"Ready, they replied softly. Harald the half-cat whipped out his sword, then silently charged across the courtyard, his troops close behind him. All eyes were turned towards the forest waiting, when suddenly Harald was among them, roaring his battle song in Old Anglo Saxon.

With Gudrun's return, Ella knew the electronics were down. It was now safe to remove the collars from the children. Shivering in the cold, she set about the task. As soon as the last one was free she shimmered back into the cat. They all went wolf and waited by her side. They could hear the king's battle song and it terrified them, but they felt safe behind the tigress. They already knew who she was. Igor had told them.

Back on the mainland, Kylie was cursing savagely under her breath. She couldn't see a damned thing in this fog and the heavy mist was soaking through her clothes. She had to do something. Taking the child by the hand she descended from her perch on the hill to the road below.

They crept ahead until she could see the drawbridge through the mist. They were right at the edge of the land.

As they crouched there she felt the child shiver beside her. "Change into the wolf," she whispered as she gave the girl's hand a squeeze. "She won't mind the cold so much." The child got the idea, gave a soft giggle, then dropped her cloak and shimmered into the wolf cub. She licked Kylie's cheek then snuggled closer.

The mist deepened and swirled across Kylie's vision, obscuring the view of the drawbridge for a moment. She knew then she had to change the plan somewhat. As the bridge came back into view she could see it was primarily made of wood. She reached for the rocket launcher just as she heard the flash bomb go off.

Moments later the sound of Harald's war song came to her just as the bridge started to move. She fired the rocket as the bridge disappeared into the mists. They were a bit too close for comfort when the shell hit the bridge. The wood was shattered into a million flying slivers, many of which fell on them. They also were momentarily blinded by the flash of light and deafened by the explosion.

The young wolf was the first to recover. She grabbed Kylie's sleeve and began to pull her back and away. Kylie allowed herself to be led away by Nikka. As soon as her head cleared she looked back. A momentary swirl in the mists showed her the shattered bridge.

No one would be crossing that this night. There would be no vehicles to worry about. Now all they had to do was wait. If anyone escaped the carnage on the island they would be on foot. Even if she couldn't see them, the young wolf would be able to hear them and show her where they were.

Back inside the compound, the battle raged. Stephan Krebs sat in his car, swearing in a dozen languages. He'd gone to his car and prepared to make a run for it as soon as the attack came. He was almost to the bridge when it shattered, raining wood and twisted metal down on his sleek new Jaguar. He wasn't going anywhere. Damn that Eric to hell and back.

Leaping from the now useless automobile, Stephan ran zig-zag back towards the apartment. At first he started toward the dog pens, but that damned tiger was there with the wolves. There would be no help from that angle. He almost stopped in shock as he first caught a glimpse of a huge man/beast wielding a broad sword with great effect.

As he turned from that apparition he saw her. Ariel! She was smooth and beautiful as ever and twice as deadly. An icy fear gripped his heart, and he fled in the opposite direction.

There were nearly thirty men in the compound, all heavily armed. It made no difference. At the sudden battle roar behind them they turned from trying to peer into the gloom to face this new challenge. It was a nightmare from hell swinging a huge broad sword. Several others like it also tore into them. The suddenness of the attack did its job. Several were dead or down before the shock wore off and the began to return fire.

At that point a pack of ravening wolves charged from the trees led by a human madman. There was also gunfire from the humans following the swordsman. Krebs' henchmen broke and tried to flee. Running blindly into the heavy fog, they sought any avenue of escape, or any place at all to hide. Several actually made it into the trees, but it didn't help; they could hear the wolves hunting them.

"Hunt them, find them," roared Harald. "Let none escape. Find them all. Gudrun, find Krebs. Bring him down."

"This way," declared Terry as he started off towards the office and apartment.

"Are you certain."

"I am, Blondie. He saw you. He got one look at you and nearly crapped his pants. He went this way."

"Good work, Terry, I've got his scent now." She ran past him with Eric close behind.

When they reached the doors they found them open. There was no gunfire to greet them. Gudrun stopped to listen and test the air. She could smell him, especially his fear. The man was terrified. He would be at his most dangerous now. As she ghosted into the outer foyer, she noticed that Terry had disappeared. Following the scent, she and Eric moved silently across the room to a door on the other side.

Outside, Harald was organizing the hunt for the fleeing men. Ella had shimmered back into a woman as he approached. He shimmered back into human form then spoke gently. "Is everything under control here? Did you get them all, Mother?"

She turned to Igor who nodded. "Yes, my king, it appears we have everyone. Harald, must you kill them all? Will the compulsion not protect us just as well?"

"Sadly, Ella, I don't believe it will. I've seen some of the magic Amanda and Clyde can do. I've spoken with them at length, discussing their skills. I fear that one with their skills could, if fully determined, dig the memories out of the mind of a compelled person. One person might be laughed off, but several telling the same story might start someone thinking. I'm quite loathe to risk it.

"Shed no tears for these men, Mother. They're all hardened criminals, steeped in the ways of violence. They'll be no great loss to the world. You can see the effects of their humanity on these children."

"But so many disappearing at once. Will they not be missed? Will inquiries not be made?"

"Probably. Kylie and Terry worked wonders with that story about Gudrun being sent to America. That was what broke it open for us. Perhaps they can muster some magic surrounding this."

"Yes, of course. I should have thought of that. Agreed then. Let's clean out this nest of vipers."

"I work as we speak." He laughed as he turned back to the sounds of gunfire in the mist. "Keep them here, Ella. Keep them safe."

"As you desire, so shall it be, my king," she replied, just before she shimmered back into the great cat. She could hear the guns and the screams of terror as the wolves hunted through the small forest.

Inside the compound the vampires were being every bit as efficient as the wolves, hunting down and dispatching the enemy. Those who had lived their lives by violence and intimidation met their fate by the same rules.

Gina returned to the compound, seeking out the king. "What is it, Gina?"

"Sire, I tracked two men into a tunnel and dispatched them. The tunnel was recently collapsed at one end. If we deposit the bodies in there and collapse the roof on them..."

"Yes, no one would ever discover what has happened here. This place is quite isolated. It could be weeks before anyone comes this way. Once they do, they will discover signs of a struggle here, but no bodies. It just might work at that. Good thinking, Gina. We'll do it."

One by one the wolves began to return. They were certain none had escaped them. Harald explained the plan, and everyone set to work. Kylie had blown the drawbridge to smithereens, so none had escaped that way. Harald was pleased. He was only waiting for Gudrun to report in.

Gudrun and Eric entered the inner office warily, he going left and she moving right. She could see well enough in the darkness and Eric was wearing night vision goggles. Suddenly strong light flashed on, effectively blinding Eric. He howled in agony and surprise as he whipped the goggles off, but it was too late. Something struck the back of his head stunning him. He sank to the floor and Stephan Krebs kicked the weapons away.

Stephan stood facing Gudrun, marvelling at her. She had raised her weapon as well, but the light had momentarily blinded her, too. He had the advantage for the moment. She lowered her gun. "Ariel, is that truly you?"

"It is I, Stephan. Who did you think was after you?"

"In truth, I imagined it was this moron." For emphasis he kicked the fallen Eric who groaned as consciousness slowly returned. "I should've known better. I do have a few questions for you, Ariel. How did you do it? How did you escape the flames?"

"I have my ways."

"Yes, you certainly do. I must admit, the woman you sent to call me was a superb likeness. I actually believed it was you."

"Actually, it was me."

"Yes, yes, have your fun while you can, Ariel. Tell me what you did to Marco. I know even Marco could be brought down with a tranquilizer dart, but it's the drugs of forgetfulness that intrigue me. What is it? Where did you get it?"

"You wouldn't believe me if I told you, Stephan."

"So you won't talk. No matter, I have other ways of finding out these things. So why did you come after me? Who could have paid you enough to come after me?"

"Ah, Stephan, as egocentric as ever. What makes you think I came after you? I came for the wolf cubs."

"What??? Who could have known about them and paid you enough to retrieve them?"

"Believe it or not, my mother."

"Your mother." Stephan was having trouble now. As usual this woman was spinning his head around. He had to regain the upper hand in the conversation. "Still the same Ariel, everything in life is a joke, an amusement. Tell me why, Ariel. I tried to make you see the big picture, but this simpering fool at my feet was ever at your ear, spreading lies about me, poisoning your mind against me. Why did you always believe him. Why would you never listen to me?

"We two together could rule the world, Ariel. None could stand before us. As I always tried to make you understand, we are a violent species. Only through violence can we attain the control to bring a lasting peace. Join me, Ariel. I have nearly achieved the control I need. A few more months and all will under my hand. We can then bring the nations to their knees, bring them under the yoke. There will be peace, Ariel. No more wars..."

"So what do the wolves have to do with it?" Gudrun had an amused smile as she spoke with him, holding his attention. She could see Eric reviving, biding his time, watching for an opening. Better yet, she sensed Terry near.

"Those abominations? Oh Ariel, they were a true gift from a benevolent god. You see, you assassinate a man or a member of his family, no matter how violently you do it, he will seek revenge. Even if he doesn't, others will try to take his place. They will fight you.

"However, kill his young children by supernatural means, you demoralize him and everyone he knows completely. Those disgusting animals took years off my projected timelines. A few more kills and all will be mine."

"But they recently began to fail, didn't they?"

"Yes, but as soon as you surfaced, I understood why. How did you know? How did you stop them?"

"We caught one by accident; the story came out then. The thing that intrigues me, Stephan, is, how did you discover them in the first place?"

"It was quite by accident, really. I was in Russia, under the guise of a film director looking for new talent. A man came to me with a film he had shot. He was some sort of naturalist. He'd been out in the mountains for years shooting film of wolves and such. He showed me his proof that werewolves were real. He wanted fortunes for the film so I could use it in my movies.

"The thing that attracted me was the speed and savagery of the kill and the feeding. I became convinced that he was telling the truth, so I set about capturing them. Oh, not all of them, but more than enough for my purposes. I fully expected the original assassins to be hunted down and killed. That's why I'm having the young whelps properly trained. Trained to kill on command and to complete obedience.

"Ariel, this is the path. We can take control of this world. We can stop the wars. Come with me; forget this fool. We can stop the wars, Ariel, all of them."

"But I don't want to stop the wars, Stephan. Wars are how I make my living, after all."

"Be serious, Ariel. For once, be serious."

"She is," grunted Eric, drawing another kick. He almost grinned as the blow landed. He'd drawn Krebs attention away from Terry who had just slipped through another door.

Krebs started to speak, but he was tackled from the side by a hurricane. His weapon was stripped away and he was knocked to the ground, but he was back up again in a heartbeat, blocking blows and delivering his own. "So, the American merc, I take it. You fool, I can eat you for breakfast."

Stephan lost his bravado as Terry's next blow took the air from his lungs momentarily. He fought back, but the shorter man was wearing him down. He grudgingly admitted to himself that this man was a match for Marco. He renewed his attack, but to no avail as the shorter man prevailed. Terry managed to get under Stephan's reach, deal a hard kick to the side of the knee then get behind him and apply a choke hold that couldn't be broken.

"Are you still breathing?" demanded Terry, as he shook his victim like a rat. "Are you?"

"Of course I'm breathing, you moron." Krebs struggled, but knew it was useless. One hard twist and his neck would be broken.

"Do you know why you're still breathing?"

"I'm sure you are going to inform me of a more terrifying doom."

"No, I'm not," said Terry as he thrust Krebs to the floor and stood back from him. "She is."

Stephan looked back to Gudrun who just smiled. "Happy Terry?"

"It'll do, Miss Gudrun. I'd rather kill him, but it'll do. He's all yours."

"Stephan," she cooed, "you have so many questions. I will now give you the answers." She shimmered into the half cat, her fangs gleaming in the light. He fell back, horrified.

"What's the matter, Stephan?" chuckled Eric. "Never seen a vampire before?"

Stephan Krebs tried to scramble to his feet, but she was on him in a heartbeat. With one hand on his throat she held him in the air, his feet not touching the floor. "I like the wars'" Her voice was soft, an almost seductive purr. "They keep me amused. I sought the wolf pups because the king wants them returned. I came after you because you burned me.

"You hurt someone special to me and you burned me, Stephan. For that I will kill you. You wanted to know what happened to Marco. This is it." Before she could put Stephan under the compulsion the wall burst inward in a cloud of flying rubble and dust. Three men charged in with guns blazing, but Eric was still on the ground, below their fire. He returned fire and they lay dead on the floor.

As Eric gunned down the enemy, Gudrun tried to find Terry. He'd been buried in the rubble. "Never mind me, get Krebs. He went that way." With a nod she set out after him but stumbled and nearly fell down the hidden stairs. They were a-swirl in a cloud of dust. Once free of the dust cloud her night vision was able to discover the way.

Gudrun came leaping down the stairs in time to hear the engine of the hidden jet ski fire up. He raced away from the island and into the heavy fog. She was in the water, swimming hard, but even in vampire form she couldn't catch the jet ski. Stephan Krebs has escaped her revenge. Worse yet, he'd seen her as the vampire.

Clean Up

The mists were getting heavier and were now a soft yet cold rain. Kylie shivered. The young wolf snuggled closer, sharing her warmth. "Thank you, Nikka," whispered Kylie, "but we need to get out of this rain. I haven't heard anything from the castle for a while now. Can you?" In response, the animal went on alert.

Peering through the mist, Kylie made out vague shadows leaving the castle through the hole in the wall where she'd blown the drawbridge to hell. With shaking hands, she readied her weapon as the figures dropped into the waters, swam ashore and began scrambling up the bank. As the first one appeared she pulled the trigger.

Nikka knocked the rifle up so the shot went high into the air. Kylie shrieked in surprise then jerked away from the wolf and tried to take aim again. There was no time. The sabertooth was on her, batting away the rifle and holding her down. Suddenly bursting into tears of relief and shivering uncontrollably from the cold and damp, Kylie wrapped her arms around the tiger's neck and clung to her.

The mighty tigress knelt and Kylie slowly crawled onto her back, digging her hands deep into the fur around her neck. The beast set out at a trot; a pack of two dozen wolf cubs followed close behind. There was no need for stealth now; Ella hurried toward the small camp.

Within an hour the three camping tents were full of wolves huddled together to share body heat while Ella, now back in human form, and Kylie snuggled in with several wolves who remained in wolf form. They would be warmer that way. The rain stopped, the mist burned off, and the sun was high in the sky before the others returned.

143

"I CAN SEE BY THAT LOOK on your face that you weren't successful, Gudrun." Harald sighed. "What happened?"

"He isn't dead, my king," she replied, "yet. I found no others within the building."

"I found two more, hiding out," put in Terry. "I dealt with it."

"Well done, people. It appears Stephan Krebs is the lone survivor. We're carrying the bodies of the fallen to a cave that once led to an escape route. It has been sealed off at one end. Once the bodies are inside we will collapse the rest of it. Vassily says he has enough explosives to accomplish the task.

"Now we have another problem, one I should have considered earlier."

"What's that?" asked Terry.

"We have wounded," replied Harald. "The wolves don't heal as we do."

"There are medical supplies on the plane," said Eric. "Jimmy has medical training. He was a military medic when we recruited him."

"They're over near the drawbridge. Bring him there." Harald turned and signalled with his arm. A huge wolf trotted over and shimmered into Olla. "Olla, find Jimmy and take him to the wounded, then help him if you can."

"The pups..."

"Ella has taken them back to our camp. They're safe, Olla." She nodded then shimmered back to the wolf. Her nose tested the air for a moment then she trotted off. She soon returned, Jimmy trotting along behind as she led him to the wounded.

"Gina!"

The small pixie of a woman came to them. "Yes, my king?"

"How are Marlene and Abel doing?"

"They are reviving nicely, Harald. They are in the trees now, locating and draining the wounded hiding there. Illya is with them, helping to sniff them out."

"Then all is well. Eric, can you land that magic plane of yours anywhere near?"

"I don't believe so, Sire. It's too tight here. I can set down near the camp in the hills though."

"Make it so, my friend. We'll be finished here soon enough. Meet us at the camp. Do you have enough fuel to get us home to America?"

"We do. I topped her up outside Glasgow before we arrived. We can go straight back to base from here."

"Excellent, excellent. The sooner we get out of this rain the happier I'll be."

"I thought you enjoyed the water, Harald." Gudrun grinned as Eric trotted away. "Eric, watch out Kylie doesn't shoot you." His laughter floated back to them as he disappeared through the hole at the drawbridge.

"I do enjoy the water, Gudrun, but not like this," sighed Harald. "This is cold, soaking through everything. We've fought hard, taken wounds, and our allies don't heal as we do. Terry's shivering hard now and some of the wolves are huddling for warmth."

"Let's get them all inside out of the weather," she replied. "Terry, take them back to that office and crank up the heat. I'll get the electricity back up for you." He nodded and went to where Jimmy was working on the wounded. Gina and Harald came to help carry those who couldn't walk.

While they worked Harald leaned close to Gudrun. "Once we have everyone safely back at headquarters, I want you to track down this Stephan Krebs and make doubly certain he's dead."

"Yes, my king. I won't fail you again."

"You didn't fail me this time, Gudrun. You engineered a complete success. Only that madman escaped us. It was more than I dared hope for. However, if you can find him..."

"I'll find him, Harald. I'm not finished with Stephan Krebs yet. Not by half." Harald nodded his approval and led her towards the shelter.

Night slowly turned to day, the rain stopped, and the sun began to burn away the mist. They fashioned a stretcher to carry the one who could not walk on his own. The tide receded and they set out. It was a long tired trudge in the sunlight. The vampires weren't happy about that, but there was little choice. At least they were well fed. By nightfall they were on a plane headed for home.

It was a tight fit in that plane, everybody jammed in on top of each other. Harald was concerned. The wolves might love this tight pack closeness, but the vampires didn't. Suddenly afraid they might lose control in mid air; he made his way to the cockpit. He expressed his concern to Gudrun who was in the co-pilot's seat.

Eric just chuckled at that. "Relax, my king," smiled Gudrun. "I've already made other arrangements to get us home. We'll be setting down in five minutes. There's an old troop carrier waiting for us at Glasgow. One of our people will pick up this plane and return it to Germany."

They landed at the airport and taxied into an older freight hangar. There was no one around when they switched to the second plane, a far older and less comfortable transport, but they could now spread out a bit. The vampires seated themselves further apart, interspersed among the shapeshifters. That move greatly relieved the tension. It was a long ride across the ocean, a stop off to refuel in Newfoundland, and then finally to the old airport outside New York. A bus was waiting.

Reunion

They got off the bus and there was a committee there to greet them. Everyone was waiting to welcome them home, especially the shapeshifters. The children, dressed in whatever clothes they had managed to find as they fled their prison, were surrounded, hugged, loved, poked, and prodded to make sure they were real and safe. In return they wept as they buried themselves in the arms of their families. All except two.

Tikka and Jan clung to Olla's leg, clinging to their mother for protection in this strange place. She had her arms around their shoulders defensively, defiantly. She squared her shoulders as Tommy approached. Everyone suddenly went quiet, sensing the tension in the air, watching to see what would happen. A wolf mates for life, but not necessarily a human.

Tommy gave Olla a big smile of welcome home as he approached. Sally had already told him Olla had found her youngest two children alive. He'd had plenty of time to prepare himself, and he knew they didn't speak English. In truth, he was a bit excited about meeting them. He had no idea at all what to do with children, but he was sure Olla could teach him. Right now it was time to make friends and keep peace in the family.

As he reached them, Tommy sat on the floor at Olla's feet. He pointed a finger at the girl. "Tikka." She nodded shyly and hid her face in her mother's side. "Jan." The boy nodded, watching Tommy carefully with wide eyes. They had been told he was their new father, but their prior experience with humans made them fearful. He pointed his thumb at his own chest. "Tommy."

Tommy took a bar from his pocket and peeled it open. Breaking off a corner, he popped it in his mouth and smiled. "Mmm, chocolate." He

147

held out the sweet treat and, with Olla's gentle encouragement, Tikka accepted the gift and tasted it. Her eyes widened with delight. Tommy produced another for Jan, then rose to his feet to face Olla.

"Welcome home, my love," he breathed in her ear, as he hugged her tightly. "It's okay now, I've got all the fur balls vacuumed from the floor."

Olla burst into laughter as she returned his hug fiercely, her heart singing with joy. Her new mate had accepted her pups, they wouldn't be sent away. "You're a crazy man, my Tommy." She laughed with delight, then kissed him deeply.

A wave of relief swept through the room as everyone else relaxed. "Well done, Tommy," said Amanda. She and Clyde had been helping him for the past couple of days. Poor Tommy had been terrified of messing up the first meeting with Olla's children, if she found them alive. They had also helped him understand what he might have to do for her if she didn't. Clyde also nodded his approval.

While Olla tried to help her children get to know and accept Tommy, Illya left Anna fussing over the children and approached the king who was gently hugging his queen. "King Harald, I have no words to express my gratitude for all you have done. May I ask what will happen to us now? Where will we go? What will become of my people?"

Harald put his hand on the man's shoulder and smiled. "The battle is won, Illya. Now we eat and drink our fill, and then we rest for a few days. Take time to properly reunite your people, rest them. In a few days we'll all gather together to discuss how we can help you return to your homes."

Disappointment

Three days passed, during which the shapeshifters united with the lost children. Amanda and Clyde offered to help with breaking the children free of Krebs conditioning and the parents were grateful. It also took three days to shake off the jet lag suffered by humans, vampires, and werewolves alike. On the fourth day they met in the conference room. Everyone was there, just waiting for the royal couple.

"All rise." That was Peter's deep basso.

Harald entered with Sally on his arm. He seated her to the right of his official chair, then sat himself. "Be seated." There was a shuffling of chairs then everyone was ready.

Harald smiled as he gazed around the long table. "I see everyone's anxious to get to it, so let's begin. We were successful in retrieving the young of Illya's people. However, I'm curious if we were as successful in covering our own tracks. Tommy, have you heard anything about our adventures in Scotland?"

"No, Sire. Not a peep."

"Kylie?"

"Nothing, Sire."

"Terry?"

"All's quiet as far as I can see."

"Good. That much is a relief. Is there any sign of Krebs?"

"Nope," sighed Terry. "Not a squeak there either."

"Damn. All right, on to the next piece of the business. Illya, may I assume you speak for the Children of the Wolf?"

"Yes, Great King. Once there were three packs and three alphas. The others are dead and few enough of our people remain. I have been accepted as the one alpha."

149

"Good. You're a wise leader and your people will need that as they rebuild the clans. So, tell me what you would like to see happen next."

"We would like to go home, King Harald. It will be hard to go back where so many were killed, but what else can we do?"

"Yes, and I did promise to make that happen for you. However, Sally would like to speak to you about this."

Sally reached across the table and laid her hand on Illya's. Her eyes went out of focus for a moment then returned. She patted his hand sadly and sat back. "Last night I dreamed of your home village, at least I thought it might be. This confirms it. There are people there, wearing modern clothing, but I have no idea who they are or what they're doing."

"Modern people." Illya sighed deeply. "Then we're finished. If they were some of our own who had managed to survive they wouldn't be wearing modern clothing. Our homes have been discovered. We are undone.

"As alpha of the pack it's my duty to fight for and protect my people. If we can get close to these people without being seen, perhaps we can drive them away. However, if we do that they may simply return in greater numbers and with modern weapons as Krebs did.

"King Harald, I can't help my people in this world that has found us. I don't know how. Will you accept them into your pack? If so, I will find the place where Owan fell and join him. I will be no threat to you."

Harald's jaw hardened and he sat back in his chair. Sally patted his arm, giving him a pleading look. With a resigned sigh, Harald allowed his posture to relax. "This is what I feared," he said. "This is what I did not, and don't want. Illya, the Children of the Wolf are strong and courageous. If this becomes the only answer I will accept your people, but only if you promise to remain with them to help and advise me. However, I'd prefer you as independent allies."

"We won't be able to survive, Great King. You know this to be true. Perhaps when the young are grown and have learned the ways of this world, but until then..." Illya left that hanging as he shrugged his shoulders. He knew the vampires to be immortal, so the time would be only a blink for them, but it would buy his people a dozen years or more. A chance to adapt to a new and more dangerous world.

Harald showed no emotion at all as he stared at Illya for a long moment. The entire room held its breath, waiting for him to respond. The merriment began in his eyes then a grin touched his lips. "So, you're a sharp negotiator, are you?" He chuckled softly. "Manoeuvred me into that pretty easily, didn't you? All right, Illya, you win. It is the best solution and I know it.

"Very well then, my sly friend, we'll hold safe and protect your people for a time of twenty years. Our people will help educate the young shapeshifters to the ways of the technological world. We'll all work together to create a way for our peoples to survive in these rapidly changing times. Do you accept?"

"We accept."

"Done then. All right people, opinions, suggestions? Gudrun?"

She arose with liquid grace and began to pace about the room. "Opinion. The mission isn't finished, Harald. Yes, we accomplished the first objective. We retrieved the children. However, we didn't eliminate the primary target. Stephan Krebs is not yet dead.

"However, once Stephan became aware of me, he got sloppy. He involved too many people as he moved the children around. We need to clear that back trail. We need to find and eliminate Stephan."

"Hold still, Gudrun, you're making me dizzy. All right, take your people and clear that trail. Kill only as absolutely necessary, but get it done."

"As you wish, my king."

"Gudrun."

"Yes?"

"I apologize. You know what must be done and the best way to do it. Just ignore my fussing and do what you need to do."

"Yes, my king." She grinned and winked at Terry. "Eric, Jimmy, Vassily, departure in ten. Gina, I'll need you to locate Marco and bring him to me. He'll have all the information I need. Terry, I'll need you to keep an eye on the king while I'm gone."

"I'll do my best, Blondie." He smiled as Harald shook his head and pointed at the door.

Laughing, Gudrun made her exit. She stopped only long enough to give Terry a searing kiss. "Don't forget me." She laughed with delight at his look of bedazzled shock. She ran from the room.

"That woman is so cold and efficient," mused Illya, "and yet so full of life. You're a lucky man, friend Terry."

"I'm a tormented man, Illya," said Terry, "but I enjoy it. Sire, I get the idea you have a task for me."

"I do, Terry. You and your team see what you can do to find us an alternate plan for the People of the Wolf. If we can't take them to their traditional home we'll need a back up plan."

"Yes, Sir, I'll be happy to take that on. May I borrow Queen Sally to assist?"

"Oh yes, I insist," said Sally. "I do want to help."

"Okay, team, let's retire to Amanda's office and put our heads together. Tommy, bring Olla with you, we'll need her input."

Once they had filed out, Harald turned back to those who remained. "Clyde, you didn't join your team."

"Nope."

"You have something else in mind?"

"I do, Sire. We seem to have guests for a while longer. With Georg and Anna's help I'd like to continue working with the children, perhaps establish a makeshift school as well. At least until things get sorted out a bit."

"I like it, Clyde. Do what you feel is best with my blessing. Now, Peter, you take Illya and whoever else you need. Hitch a ride with

Gudrun to Europe, return to the village. Find out what the hell is going on there and do what you must to muddy the waters."

"Understood, Harald. Come, Illya, my old friend. We will return together."

Soon the vast room was empty except for Harald and the remaining vampires. "I see that smug smile of yours, Ella. Tell me."

"I was just patting myself on the back for being wise enough to appoint you king, Harald. You're so good at it."

"Yes, yes, I know, I was born to it. Have your fun, Mother."

"But, you have a task for me?"

"I do, all of you. There's been far too much activity around here of late. Too much food being brought into the building, too many delivery trucks coming and going, etc."

"And you want us to make sure there are no curious people prowling around."

"Yes, people, that's what I want. From now until we have the Illya's people established in a new home we need to redouble our efforts with our own security. Yes, I know Tommy has his electronics constantly scanning the area and the building is alarmed and more...but..."

"Tommy's machines failed us once before," said Ella, a hard edge in her voice. "They're incredibly useful, but not infallible. We'll add our skills to the mix. Come children, let us devise a system of constant patrols to carry us through this time of flux. Jakob, you've been keeping an eye on things, give us your thoughts."

Harald sighed and sank back into his chair. This was the part of being king that he had always hated. Everyone was busy at their tasks and all he could do now was wait, depend on them to get it done, and hope he'd covered all the possibilities. Perhaps he would kill a few hours in the gym with sword practice.

THE SHAKEN AND BENT man shuffled back towards his tiny room in the ancient hotel. It had been a long day, and he was tired. Even though he told himself he'd done well, serving the needs of the homeless, something gnawed at him. A black murderous rage chewed at him, his thoughts, but he had control of it.

He told himself it was the madness that had driven him to this lot in life. He had to make up for those thoughts by doing good deeds. But the fear, deep inside him laughed at him and a woman of darkness haunted his dreams. Above all else Marco was afraid and he didn't know why.

Before he could enter the doors, a van pulled up beside him and two men in military uniform grabbed him and hauled him inside, as the van raced away. He cowered in the seat, but they only smiled at him and offered him an energy bar and water. When the vehicle finally stopped, the men helped him out.

He was in a warehouse and two women were waiting for them. Marco tried to hide behind the men. There was the woman of darkness. He was terrified of her and a part of him wanted to kill her.

The woman of his dark and fearful dreams stepped forward. She spoke in a voice from a hell he could not name. "*Marco, remember.*"

It took a few moments then all his memories came flooding back. "You!"

"Me." She smiled delightedly.

"You, you're the one Stephan wanted me to kill," he said as he faced Gudrun. "You're like that one. That's why you can't be killed. Stephan will figure it out. He'll find a way to finish you."

"Stephan will soon be dead by my hand," she replied coldly.

He met her eyes for a long moment then sighed. "I believe you. Am I now to precede my friend into the mystery?"

"Not yet," replied Gudrun. "We have some questions for you."

Marco held up his hand protectively. "Don't. Don't do that thing to me. I'll tell you whatever you want to know. Just kill me cleanly afterwards. Don't do that thing to me again."

"You loved him, didn't you?" said Gina as she stepped closer.

"Yes, somewhat, in a strange sort of way. For all the good it did me. Stephan prefers women, at least one woman. Her. I'll answer your questions, but may I ask, how did he escape you? I assume he has, or you wouldn't have come for me again."

"Stephan has always been slippery as an eel," replied Gudrun. "We're wasting time here. Tell me everywhere you took the wolf cubs after they were captured. Give me the names of everyone who was aware of them. Tell me this for every location including the last one in Scotland."

"It'll do you no good at all." He sighed as he sank to a seat in the opening of the van. "They're too many and will be scattered now."

"Could you find them?"

"I could, maybe, but..."

"Gudrun, he'll be useless for this purpose under the compulsion. There's only one way to be certain..."

"Are you serious? Gina, you know what this'll do to you in the end?"

"Yes, I know. Call it my payback for returning me to life after Mobutu tortured and killed me. Besides, I like him, Gudrun. You know I have a thing for bad boys." Suddenly Gina swallowed hard and took a step back from Gudrun. Murder danced in those cold blue eyes.

"If I even think this might go sideways," Gudrun said softly, "I'll kill you both. Do you understand, Gina?"

"I'll keep a tight reign on him, Gudrun, I promise." Gudrun gave a curt nod of her head and Gina relaxed slightly. She realized Gudrun meant what she'd said and had no desire to push her luck that far. "If they're scattered far and wide we need him alert. He'll be useless under the compulsion."

"All right, you've won your point. Get on with it. We're wasting time."

Gina turned to Marco and crooked her finger. "You're not going to do that voice thing again, are you?"

"No, Marco. I won't do that to you again. However, I do need you to help us, and I need you to behave. Come to me now."

He stood and approached her, not knowing what to expect. She leaped on him, knocking him to the ground with her atop him. Her fangs bit deep for a moment then she stopped and licked the wound on his throat. She bit her own wrist and gave him the tiniest taste of her blood then sealed that wound as well. "What's happening to me? What did you do?" he asked as she helped him to his feet.

"I've marked you as my own. You want to be mine, don't you?"

"Of course I do," he replied, "but I don't understand what's happening."

"It's all right. I gave you a taste of my blood to help you heal faster." Her voice was a soft purr. "Come with us. We need to talk to all your old friends in Europe. You can help us find them, can't you Marco?"

"Of course I can. Whatever you want, lady, I'll be happy to do."

"Come then. We must be off."

Gudrun sat brooding in the co-pilot's seat as the plane sped over the vast ocean. "When this is finished we'll have to kill him," Eric said softly.

"Hush, she'll hear you," whispered Gudrun, "but you're right. It would be too cruel to put him under the compulsion again. That longing for her would never be silenced, not even by the compulsion."

"When the time comes, I'll do it."

"No, Eric, when the time comes, she'll do it. This I promise you."

In the passenger's area of the plane, Gina continued to smile at Marco who was fawning over her. She'd heard everything. "Yes I will, my sister," she sighed to herself. "Unless I can find a way to keep him alive and return him to the magnificent specimen he once was. I can shift his complete devotion to me, I know I can. There's no way he can hold anything back, not from me. Not now."

FAR AWAY TO THE NORTHEAST, Stephan Krebs worked diligently at his task. The captain of the fishing boat that had rescued him was a harsh man. They had landed in the Faroe Islands, but Stephan had been unable to access his bank accounts. He'd been unable to fulfill his promise to the man. As a result he'd been forced to work off the money owed. No matter, it would get him to Norway. As soon as he contacted his people all would be well. And the captain would be dead.

Return to the Mountains

"You don't like the flying machines, Peter?" Illya grinned as the rental car sped down the highway towards the mountains and his distant home.

Peter was behind the wheel and smiling for the first time since they'd boarded the plane for Russia. "Why do you say that, Illya?"

"Because you're smiling now, and I can no longer smell your fear."

Peter's deep rumbling laugh brought a smile to his companion's face. "All right, I'll confess it. I hate flying."

"But your people cannot die, Peter. What is there to fear?"

"The heights. I like my feet firmly planted on the ground."

Georg chuckled from the back seat. His life was good again. His children were alive and safely back under the care of the vampire king, and he was nearing his beloved mountains for the first time in over a year. In a very few days they would be home again. He prayed that the queen had been mistaken and that it would be safe to return. He was only deluding himself. Deep down inside, he knew she was right. They could never go home.

Three days later they arrived at the village. There were people everywhere. A makeshift road had actually been punched through the mountains to the village.

"What is going on here?" Peter demanded in Russian as he strode towards a knot of excited people.

"We've discovered something wonderful," replied one woman. She seemed to be the one in charge. "After the death of an old friend I was gifted with his field notes. Sadly, much of it was the ramblings of a madman, but his directions to this place were remarkably good.

"What he'd actually found was a living tribe of humans thought to be extinct for over eighty thousand years. These people were neither

158

homo sapiens nor Neanderthals, but something else entirely. How they have managed to remain hidden in these mountains until now, no one knows."

"Where are they?" asked Peter.

"We don't know. Their homes are empty, but they look so lived in. It's like something happened about a year ago and they just abandoned the place en mass. We found several graves about a day away and we are working up the DNA profile now."

"You disturbed the bodies?" asked Illya, a dangerous note in his voice.

The woman was oblivious to the danger. "Of course. To find such perfect specimens is a god send. We...wait, just who are you people and by what right do you question me?"

"I'm your new supervisor," replied Peter. "Call all your people over here right now. I wish to speak with them." Reluctantly she obeyed. "Is this everyone?"

"Yes."

"Excellent. *Hear me. Obey me. What you have found here is an elaborate hoax. This is all fake. You will now pack up everything and return to your homes.*"

It took only a moment for it to settle in then there began much complaining about the lengths some people would go to create a hoax. "Those bodies must have been stolen," said Peter. "Tell me who has them and where they are. I'll take care of all unpleasantness."

"Thank you," replied the woman. She wrote down the information for him then went to pack up her equipment.

Peter walked aside, out of hearing, then called Harald. He gave a full report, including the compulsion he had used. "Nicely done, Peter. Can you follow through and clear up the rest?"

"I can, Sire. I also want to return the bodies to their graves."

"Do what you must, Peter then return to us. Take whatever time you need."

"Thank you, Harald. I'll be as swift as I can." He tucked the phone back into the pocket of his coat and returned to Illya. "Once they're gone we'll burn it all."

"Yes, I can see that's the only way, Peter. Do we wait for them to leave?"

"No, we must find and retrieve the bodies of your kin. We'll return your dead to their forest then burn the houses."

"Yes, and after that we should go back to the king and see what he wants to do from there."

"That is the wisest course," agreed Peter. "We'll finish here, then return to the west. This is no longer a safe home for you. We must find another."

"NOW, GO SIT IN THE park and count to 100. After that go about your business as usual." Gina watched the man walk away then turned to her companions. "I believe that's the last of them, Gudrun. That was the last one here, wasn't it, Marco my love?"

"Yes, Mistress. Only those in Russia remain."

"How many are there?"

"Only three. All the others went with us to Scotland."

"And there's no sign of Stephan having been here?"

"No, Lady. He hasn't been here since we left with the wolf pups."

Gudrun nodded then reached for her phone. "Warm her up, Eric. We're going to Russia to finish this."

"Warming her up. Looking forward to getting back to the King's court?"

"Actually I am, and if you say a word about Terry, I'll shoot you myself." She smiled and broke the connection at his bellow of laughter.

"You like Eric, don't you Gudrun."

"I do," she replied, as she tossed a backpack to Marco, then unlocked the car. He stowed it in the trunk before occupying the back seat.

"So, why Terry and not Eric?" asked Gina, as she slid in on the passenger's side.

Gudrun sighed and let her shoulders slump. "Hard to say, Gina. I could give you a dozen reasons. They'd all sound reasonable, but the truth is, I really don't know. Let me ask you this, why him?" She jerked her thumb at the man in the back seat.

"As you say, my sister. I really have no idea."

"You know he's homosexual, bi-sexual at best."

"Yes, well, I will admit, that does complicate things somewhat. However, I've claimed him. He will never betray us. Even he couldn't overcome that."

"You've done this before, haven't you?"

"Call me a sick woman, but I sometimes find unrequited love to be a real delight, if only for a short time."

"Don't kill me," came a soft voice from the back seat. "I can be useful to you. I have skills."

"You've said those words before, haven't you, dear?" Gina smiled as she turned to him.

"Yes. I asked Stephan not to shoot me. I promised to serve him well, and I did. He came to trust me, and I never once betrayed that trust, until now. Until I met you, lady, I would not have believed I would ever betray that trust. I don't understand what you've done to me."

"You like it, don't you Marco? You like me better than Stephan, don't you?"

"I would kill Stephan himself for you, lady. I swear it. Don't kill me. I can be useful to you."

"We'll take you to the king," said Gudrun. "He will decide your fate." Nothing more was said until they reached the plane. Two days later, they were on their way back to the U.S A. They still hadn't found any sign of Stephan Krebs.

A Wild Idea

"Sally, you're amazing. How did you discover this?" Amanda was shaking her head and smiling.

"Pure hokus pokus, right Sal?" Kylie was grinning and Sally shook a threatening finger at her.

"Scoff if you will, peasants, but you have to admit, it worked. First I read the cards, then did a psychic reading on that. The next day this showed up on my Facebook feed."

"You're on Facebook, Sally?"

"Yes Terry, I am. Stop being such a worry wart. I only use it from the apartment. I'm extremely careful of what I say, and Tommy monitors me carefully."

"Tommy, why didn't I know about this?"

"I gave you the memo, boss." Tommy sighed. "These accounts are leftovers from the old days of government work. I watch them carefully."

"Why don't I have one?"

"You do. You never did use it."

"Boys, boys, can we focus please. My idea. Does it check out?"

"Yes, my queen," replied Tommy. "Sorry. Yes, your idea checks out. It's true. Shall we take this to the king?"

"Let's do it. All right, I get to present it."

"Oh yes, my queen, this one is all your baby," grinned Terry.

Harald smiled with delight as he entered the conference room where the team had gathered to present their case. Sally was smiling excitedly and that made his heart soar as well. "All right, people, tell me what you've got that has my Sally so excited."

"We've found the perfect solution to the problem of a home for the wolf people," began Sally, fairly bouncing in her seat.

163

"So, don't keep me in suspense, tell me."

"Well, there's a whole town for sale right beside a national forest."

"A whole town for sale. Seriously? Why is it for sale?"

"Ghosts," said Terry.

"Ghosts? It's a ghost town?"

"Yes, and it's for sale," enthused Sally. "Tommy, maps."

"On screen," grinned Tommy, as the big screen lit up.

The images of about two dozen rundown and abandoned houses stood silently amid overgrown fields. A forest could be seen in the background. Harald sat silently as the views played out before him. The camera pulled back and there was a map of the national forest showing its size and a small yellow dot to locate the ghost town.

"Those houses need a lot of work," mused Harald. "Is there a road into the town?"

"Not for a long time," said Terry. "There's still traces of it, and I believe it is still on the books. We could probably get it fixed up a bit by the county."

"Why did you choose this option?" asked Harald as he smiled warmly at his wife.

"Two main reasons, my love. First is the nearness of a forest that doesn't allow hunting. The second is the isolation. It would be pretty hard for the curious to sneak up on our people in that place, especially if they're on their guard."

"I like your reasoning, Sally dearest. All right, people. Peter and Illya should be over their jet lag by tomorrow. Gudrun and company are already on their way back, so, we'll call a meeting for two days hence to present the proposal. With any luck, Illya will like it."

"He will," smiled Olla. "I heard him tell Georg that living in the city is his worst fear. This is the perfect solution."

"All right then, start gathering information, what will we need and what will we have to do to make this happen."

King Harald's good mood was shattered later that day as Gudrun and her crew returned. He was in the conference room with Sally's group, discussing the plans for the ghost town when Gudrun and company walked in. At sight of Marco, Olla transformed and leaped. Gudrun caught the wolf in mid leap and rolled her away. The wolf fought, but Gudrun had also transformed. In seconds she had the wolf pinned. Tommy nearly panicked. "Stop it, Olla, stop now. She'll kill you. Stop it."

"Hold," roared Harald, as he rose and swept into the mix, forcing Gina, who had transformed and was protecting Marco, back from Gudrun and the wolf. "Gudrun, Olla, Gina, human form. Now!" They obeyed, Olla glaring her hate at Marco and Gina watching her carefully.

Gudrun was still holding Olla back. "Stop now, Olla. She'll kill you, then your children will be orphans. Stop now." Slowly Olla began to relax, still glaring at Marco.

"Olla, speak," commanded Harald.

"My king, that one is the one who killed my mate. That one threw a child into a pit of dogs to be torn apart. That's Marco, Stephan's favourite slave. Let me kill him, Sire. He deserves to die in the jaws of a wolf."

"I'll rip you apart if you try," growled Gina menacingly.

"Was that a challenge, Gina?" Harald asked softly.

The blood drained from her face, and she took a step back. "No, Sire. Harald, please, listen to me. Please listen."

"You've claimed him, haven't you?"

"Yes, Sire. It was..."

"Silence. Gudrun, talk to me."

"It was the only way, Harald. Too many people had seen. Too many knew. Marco was the only link to them all. The only way to track them down in a timely manner. Gina claimed him to assure his loyalty and the truthfulness of his information."

"Accepted. However, that's not the only reason she claimed him. Is it, Gina?"

"Harald, I..."

"Don't try to lie to me, woman. I remember Spain, 1754, Madrid."

Gina fairly melted, averting her eyes from his penetrating gaze. "Please, Harald. This will be different, I promise you."

The king softened his posture, but only slightly. "It had better be, Gina. We can't afford such adventures in this day and age of electronic intrusiveness. Gudrun, tell me why that man is still alive."

"He may still be useful, Harald. Terry and his team have many contacts and useful insights into the official view of life here. Marco has been on the inside of the criminal element all his life and he was Stephan's right hand man."

In spite of himself, Harald chuckled. "I've always admired the way you can think fast on your feet, Gudrun. All right, you point's taken. Gina, you keep a tight reign on this one or, by all the gods, I will tear your head off myself. Now get him out of here and keep him away from the wolves."

Gina was actually trembling now. She knew she'd crossed the line and she knew how close she was to death. Her only options now were to leave, take Marco and go on the run, or to find a way to smooth this out right now. Running wasn't an option; Gudrun would be sent after her. She had to smooth it out.

"Harald, will you not trust me? Will you not give me this chance to redeem myself in your eyes? Spain was a long time ago. I've learned much since then. I remember how Mobutu found me and the result of that. I'm not that starry eyed youngster anymore. I know what's at stake here. Please don't send me away."

Harald met her eyes for a long moment then sighed. "Olla, advise me here. What do you think I should do?"

The phrase, "Kill him." was on her lips, but she bit it back. Tommy's arms were around her now and Ella had risen to approach.

It wasn't lost on Marco that when this tall woman moved everyone, including the king, responded with respect. He watched carefully as she approached Olla. Ella took Olla's hands gently. "Remember, Olla. Remember."

"Where's the fun without the risk?"

"Exactly," grinned Ella.

Olla looked directly at Marco. "I have done terrible things, but these people gave me another chance for a better life. I can do no less for you." Everyone let out a deep breath as the tension eased from the room. "Marco, I'll be watching."

Marco only nodded, wisely judging it was better not to speak. "So be it," sighed the king. "Gudrun, this is your mess. Teach Gina some self discipline, will you."

"That process has already begun, my king," Gudrun replied, locking her eyes on Gina and giving her head a jerk.

Gina took Marco's hand and led him behind Gudrun. She slowly let a long deep shuddering sigh escape her. That had been a lot closer than she'd expected. She hadn't counted on the wolf knowing about Marco. She silently cursed herself as Harald resumed his high seat. "Dammit, Gina, you sure can pick 'em. You have to keep Marco on a short leash or you'll both be in the soup."

The original discussion resumed at the long table with Gina and Marco sitting slightly apart and saying nothing. At this point Gina was content to be ignored and Marco was content just to be near her. He remembered everything. Stephan had promised to keep him safe, but he couldn't. Stephan had come to depend on him for safety. That would never happen with his Lady of Darkness. She would keep them both safe for she had allied herself with the true king of the world. Marco actually felt safe for the first time in his life.

Home at Last

The next day the king set out with Illya and Anna to get a first hand look at the ghost town. Travelling through the night, then hiking for hours in the sun didn't improve Harald's mood any, but the gasp of sheer delight from Anna and Illya did. "Well?" he asked.

"This place is beautiful," replied Anna. "Yes, the houses are old and falling down, but the quiet, the hills, and there's the forest. Oh, Illya, it has been so long since we ran through the trees."

"Go on, both of you," said Harald. "I'm going to find shade and get some sleep." His smile broadened as he watched the two wolves race towards the forest. A quick look around showed a front porch gracing the silent world with welcoming shade. Harald Eldredsson, the antiques dealer might be accustomed to his comforts, but Harald the Saxon was quite happy under a tree out of the burning sun. Still smiling, he headed for the old porch and the inviting shade.

It was near dawn when they returned to find him sitting by a small campfire, happily chatting on the phone with Sally. "This is a good place," declared Illya, as he shimmered back into human form.

"Then we will get things in motion."

"Great King, I have learned that most humans put great faith in money. I also imagine all you have done for us has cost you dearly. How can we ever repay you?"

"I've granted sanctuary and aid to my allies, Illya. The day may come when I ask the same of you. Until then, give that no further thought. Tommy has taken care of all that for us."

"Tommy? What did he do?"

"Well, it seems Olla called him a master thief. That gave him an idea. He worked his magic with the computers and found where Stephan Krebs hid all his money. Yes, the man who stole your children

168

has donated a vast fortune to us. It seems only fair to use it to help your people relocate here."

Illya just shook his head in bemusement. "I don't understand these things as he does. Perhaps Olla has chosen wisely at that. So, what do we do now?"

"Now we go home and set the wheels in motion," replied Harald. "Contractors will come to make the homes livable or to rebuild them. Also they will set up solar power and wind turbines for the electricity. My people will supervise them and they will not remember where they were or what they really did.

"Once the homes are ready, we'll bring your people here. Tommy will bring the equipment, help you get everything set up, and train your younger folk to manage it."

"Yes, the young ones seem to enjoy the computers."

"Indeed so. From time to time one or the other of my people will visit you to make certain all is well. We'll help educate the children as well. Also, if for any reason you have business in the city or if you just want to visit, know that you will always be welcomed at my court.

"So, let's head back and get this process under way. I expect you're anxious to get things started."

"Yes, my king," smiled Illya. "We are indeed."

All in all, it took three months to get everything set up and rolling. Through that time period Gudrun and Eric ran a boot camp for all concerned. Martial arts, combat skills, and weapons training in the mornings, tactics and computer skills were the order of the afternoons. The king's court looked more like an armed rebel camp than a royal court, but it paid off. Harald was thrilled with the results. So much so he declared a full two weeks of holidays when it came time to move the wolves into their new home.

Harald rented tour buses and the entire court went along for the ride. Two days on the road, then a three hour hike brought them to their destination. He beamed with delight as he watched the people exploring the new homes, chattering away together in a language only they could understand, then as one they stripped off and shape shifted.

As the wolf pack raced towards the forest they were joined by a sabre-toothed tiger. They all vanished into the trees together. The sun was down and it was growing dark when Ella returned. "They lost me, Harald." She laughed with delight as she swiftly pulled on the clothes Kylie handed to her. "There was no way I could keep up with them. I have no idea when they'll return."

"Ah well, it doesn't matter," he said. "We'll leave tomorrow and Tommy can stay behind with Olla for a few days until he has them all settled in." In the end, Tommy had the place to himself for two whole days before the Children of the Wolf returned.

Last Piece of the Puzzle

After they returned home, Harald slept two days away. Only Sally had known how much the entire adventure has weighed on him. It was Harald's task to keep the secret of their existence from getting out and a madman had nearly done just that. Now the job was done. The Children of the Wolf were settled in their new home, everyone who had contact with them was either under the compulsion or dead, and there was only one small loose end left to tie up.

Harald called his court to the huge meeting room, the great hall, as he called it. Everyone could sense something was up. The king leaned his elbows on the table and gazed at Gina until she started to sweat. Finally, she broke. "What?"

"What indeed?" he replied. "Do you remember what I promised you the day I granted you immortality?"

"You promised to kill me if I ever betrayed the secret of our existence. My King, I have not betrayed the secret."

"She's telling the truth, Harald," said Ella, gently patting his hand.

"Talk to me, Gina. Tell me what I need to know."

"I have claimed Marco, Sire. A full claim. He cannot betray that. Not ever."

"A full claim? Why?"

Gina sighed and slumped in her chair. "Several reasons, Sire."

"Care to share them with me?"

"We needed information. Marco was the only human left alive who knew exactly who had known of the shapeshifter. He and he alone had been in charge of getting them from Russia to Scotland."

"Would the compulsion not have worked as well without the baggage?"

171

"No, Sire. Those people were scattered and in hiding after our attack on Scotland. Under the compulsion he wouldn't volunteer any information. It could have taken years to track them all down. I assumed speed was of the utmost importance in this case."

"A compelling argument, Gina, and I do see your point. However, I get the sense there's more."

She shrugged her shoulders in defeat. "Okay, so I kind of like the guy. When we first met he put up one hell of a fight, granted me a good meal, and coughed up the information we needed. I took his memory and put him to work in a mission to help the homeless. When we went back for him and restored his memory he begged us to kill him cleanly rather than face the compulsion again."

Harald stared at his hands for a moment then slowly shook his head and chuckled. "Got you by the heartstrings like a lost puppy, didn't he?"

Gina sighed in relief. She'd been forgiven. "Yes, he did. What can I say? I'm a sucker for puppy dog eyes."

Harald turned to Gudrun. "Your assessment and recommendation?"

"He told us he had been completely loyal to Stephan. My people already confirmed that was true. He also swore he would be completely loyal to us as well. I believe him, especially since Gina's claimed him. Talk to the man, Harald. Judge for yourself."

"The thing is, he's not one of us." Everyone turned to Terry.

"Explain, Terry."

"Well, Sire, up until this point, all the humans under your rule are from my old team."

"So you think I should just kill him to be on the safe side, is that it?"

"Not at all, Sire. My point is, it'll be hard to integrate him into the inner circle. You've also invited Olla and Georg to be part of the court.

They knew quite well what Marco's role was in all this. Olla would probably kill him at the first opportunity."

"Good point. What do you suggest we do with him?"

Terry sat back and grinned wickedly, tossing a careless wink at Gina. "Boss, I think this man is a great asset. You've got us as contacts with the government. We always know what they're up to as soon as they do. The thing is, we have no contacts at all in the underworld. Also, we still have to track Stephan Krebs down. Marco could be a big help there."

Both Harald's huge hands hit the table like a clap of thunder. He sat up straight, gazing right at Terry. "By all the gods of war, you're right, Terry. It was the underworld that discovered the shapeshifters and nearly blew the whole thing wide open. We do need people on the inside. Gina, get Marco in here. I want to talk to your new boy."

Marco showed no fear at all as he entered the room. In the weeks since Gina had claimed him he had regained his former stature and had renewed all his fighting skills. He and Terry had been training together. The shorter man was a good match for him. He strode easily into the hall and stood behind Gina's chair. All the love, loyalty, and admiration he'd had for Stephan had been transferred to her now.

"The king wishes to speak with you, my darling boy," she said, patting the hand on her shoulder.

"Sire?"

"Tell me about yourself, Marco. I feel the need to know more about you."

"Yes, Sire. I was born in a prison in South America. My mother was shot, and I was given to a peasant couple. My father was abusive and at the age of ten I cut his throat and left."

"You have no regrets about the killing?"

"None, Sire. Stephan always said I was a sick man, but I'm not. He is."

"Oh?"

"I take no pleasure from the killing. I kill as needed to survive, or as directed by my employer. Stephan does."

"Yes he does," agreed Gudrun. "It's one of the reasons I let him go."

"He resented that," replied Marco, turning his attention to her. "He hated you and loved you, but mostly he feared you."

Marco turned back to Harald. "I was working for a drug cartel as an enforcer when I met Stephan. His men ambushed and defeated us. I asked him not to kill me. When he asked why he shouldn't I told him he would find no more loyal man than me. I proved that loyalty to him many times over the years."

"Tell me about that, Marco. That unquestioning loyalty. Where does that come from?"

"When I left home I was taken in and trained by a drug lord. I watched and learned as I grew up. Undying, unquestioning loyalty, is the only means of survival in that world, Sire. Ambition leads to certain death. Disloyalty the same."

"And now you're loyal to Gina."

"Completely."

"Tell me about crime in this country, Marco. Do you know who runs it? Can you get into their confidence?"

"Yes. Easily. By now they all know Stephan is in hiding. I alone was his confidante; I have all his secrets. A chance to tap into that knowledge will tempt any and all in this country."

"Excellent. Marco, you now have a new and far more dangerous employer. Me. I want you to tap into the crime world in this city. Gina, will help you. I want to keep a finger on the pulse of things around here. Most specifically, I want to make certain my people and the shapeshifters remain a secret. Should anyone suspect or start nosing around here, I want to know about it immediately."

"Understood, Sire. Will Miss Gina be directing the operation?"

"She will. Gina, set Marco up with whatever he needs. Use your persuasive skills to help things along. Oh, and keep Marco away from the wolves as much as possible."

"I will, Harald, I promise." She smiled as she rose to her feet. "Marco and I will set up an apartment someplace nearby and operate from there."

"Make it so," he smiled.

He waited until she led Marco from the room then sighed and relaxed deeply into his chair. "How did it all come to this, Mother?"

"What do you mean, Harald?" asked Ella, a smile playing at her lips.

"You know full well what I mean. A few years ago I was content in my shop in London. Suddenly you reappeared, made me king, and it's just multiplied ever since. I've gone from trying to hide nine vampires to ruling over vampires, werewolves, and god knows what else will happen along. We have our fingers into the government, a mercenary culture in Europe, and now into the American underworld."

"Want to toss it all and run away?"

"Sometimes, Ella, yes I do."

"But you can't."

"No, I cannot. Ah well, we seem to have put the final seal on this little adventure for now. Sally tells me there is only one small loose end to tie up then we can relax and get back to a semblance of normal."

"One more loose end. Stephan," growled Gudrun. "My people are hunting him even now. Have we missed something else?"

"We have missed nothing," smiled Sally. "This one is yours to deal with."

"Mine?"

"Yours," replied Sally. "Go talk to that man." She pointed right at Terry whose look of surprise spoke volumes.

"Yes, my queen. Terry, come along sweetie. We have things to discuss and arrangements to make."

"We do?" he asked as he obediently followed her towards the door.

"Yes, we do..."Just then her phone rang. With a snarl of impatience, she glanced at it. "Ah, it appears our discussion must wait. Stephan Krebs has surfaced. It seems he is on his way to America. He boarded a plane less than an hour ago. He's coming here."

"Best news I'll get today," said Terry, as he began writing a text on his phone.

"No it isn't," she grinned, "but it'll keep for now. Find that bastard for me, Terry."

STEPHAN KREBS SIGHED as he gazed out the window of the plane. His tall frame was jammed against the wall by a huge man with bad breath, a man who was determined to make small talk. Stephan studiously ignored him. He wanted to kill him.

Killing was uppermost on his mind as the plane droned onward over the cold waters below. At the top of that list was Ariel, or whatever the hell she was. Eric had called her a vampire and he believed it. He had escaped her, but she was still hunting him. Worse yet, somehow she had restored Marco and he was helping her.

After landing in Norway, Stephan had called in some old favours to get some money. Somehow Ariel had found and stolen his bank accounts. Marco, that traitorous bastard, it had to have been him. No one else knew the passwords. He had followed them across Europe, trying to figure out what they were doing as they hunted him. None of his old associates would even meet with him, and they all denied any knowledge of werewolves or vampires.

Eventually he'd stopped mentioning either of them. It only made people nervous, made them evasive. He had no idea what Ariel had done to them, but he knew it was her doing. It had to be. Her and that thrice damned Eric. They both had to die. Marco would be first though. He had to make him an example. Disloyalty could not be tolerated.

Cray would find them. He was Marco's main contact in America. He was probably already in business with Marco. He would have to approach Cray silently. Stephan was tired of depending on others to get things done for him. If you wanted something done right you had to do it yourself.

He would ambush Cray, compromise him, then lure Marco and Ariel into the trap. No more pretty traps, a bullet through the head would do the job well enough. He didn't care what Ariel was, a bullet would stop her and a stake through the heart would finish the task.

That thought was his only comfort as he tried in vain to distance himself from the bulk of his fellow passenger. Gods how he hated flying steerage. He belonged in first class.

GUDRUN AND TERRY CAUGHT up with Gina and Marco at Gina's apartment. "Gudrun, come in. What's going on? Did Harald send you? Are you here to supervise me?"

"No, no, and no, Gina. We just got word that Stephan has surfaced and is on a plane to America. No doubt he's looking for revenge. Since he's coming here I can only assume he's aware that Marco is working for us now. He'll be looking for vengeance."

"Yes, he will," said Marco. "I've tried many times to convince him that vengeance is a waste of energy and resources. He would never listen."

"Where will he go, Marco?" asked Terry. "Who will he contact?"

"Cray. He'll be Stephan's first contact if he hasn't already connected with him."

"Can this Cray be trusted?"

"No."

"Can he be bought?"

"Absolutely."

"That's our entry point," grinned Terry. "You contact Cray and offer him whatever you need to. We have to get to him before Krebs shows up."

"I can probably arrange that. May I use your phone, Miss Gina?" She tossed it to him. They all listened carefully as he arranged the meeting with Mr. Cray. He closed the connection and passed back the phone. "He'll meet with us in one hour."

"Do you know the place?"

"I do. Lady, it'll be a trap."

"Are you certain?"

"If Stephan has already spoken with him Cray will be dreaming of unlimited power here in the states. If he hasn't, then no harm done."

"Good point," said Gudrun. She dialed her phone then passed it to him. "Give Eric the location." Marco was grinning as he did so.

Final Showdown

Terry joined Gudrun and her mercenaries. He remained silent as she handed out the assignments while the van sped through the city. They passed by the appointed meeting place with everybody taking in as much as they could on a single pass. The van continued on for another city block then parked.

Gudrun turned to face her people. "All right, what did you see? Jimmy?"

"This will be a challenge to get in position, but I'll have a clear view."

"Vassily?"

"Same for me, Gudrun. It'll take me a while to get there."

"Eric?"

"My position is easier to get to, but what of the snipers we encounter? They won't be happy about giving up their positions. I should probably go first. I believe I can see Vassily's position from there. I might be able to clear his spot for him. Jimmy's too."

"Terry? Are you all right with this?"

"I am, but there's a hole in the plan. Everything hinges on Eric getting into position unobserved. I can make that easier. If I can draw their attention for a minute Eric can reach the nest unseen."

"I don't like you taking unnecessary chances, Terry."

"We can talk about that later, Blondie. Right now we're on the clock. Give me two minutes, Eric, then make your play. I'll finish my walk on the other side of the overpass."

Before Gudrun could stop him he was out of the van and moving. Her heart was in her mouth as she watched him. There were layers of highway and streets overlapped each other in a stack of three. They were on the top layer. Down on the bottom layer was the meeting place.

This part of the city was old and run down. There was no traffic at this time of night.

Terry stopped running as he reached the point where he'd be visible from the ground. He began to stagger and sing a bawdy song. As he wove his way along, nearly falling from the edge of the ramp-way, Eric raced by on the other side of the street, hidden from view below.

As Terry passed slowly by, Eric slipped below the edge of the pavement and found a sniper settled in on a huge support pillar. A powerful arm encircled the sniper's neck from behind. A quick twist, a snapping sound, and the man went limp. Eric laid him aside carefully then took his place. A quick scan showed up another sniper across the way and one layer down.

Eric took careful aim and squeezed the trigger. A soft pop from his rifle and the other sniper twitched once then was still. Vassily was moving into position when another sniper met the same fate. Jimmy moved in and readied his weapon. Terry was now across the lines of sight and had fallen silent. Down below, the meeting was about to take place. Gudrun was on the ground, ghosting toward the open space where the three cars had met.

Down on the street things were getting under way. Gina was playing the role of Marco's driver. She got out of the car then went to open the door for him. Marco stepped out dressed in an expensive suit, nodded to Gina then walked halfway between the cars. "Come on out, Mr. Cray. As you can see I'm alone except for my driver and she's obviously unarmed."

Both the other cars opened up and several armed men got out. Two of them approached Marco and patted him down. "He's clean, Mr. Cray." They withdrew back to their cars and a large man emerged from one car. He and his two bodyguards approached Marco.

"Marco, I must say, I'm surprised. First, to see you alive and in full command of your faculties, and second to see that you'd actually come alone and unarmed. You're far too trusting."

"Am I, Mr. Cray? I thought this was a negotiation in good faith."

"It is, Marco. Indeed it is. However, it's not you I'm negotiating with, you see. It is your former employer."

"My former employer? Are you saying Stephan's still alive? Forgive me if I don't believe you. The mercenaries I sent to kill him are extremely efficient."

"Oh he's alive, Marco. I spoke with him just minutes ago. He'll be right along. My men are picking him up at the airport as we speak. I'm sure he'll want to talk to you. Personally, I can't wait to see this delightful family reunion."

"All right, Cray," said Marco. "Have your fun, but indulge me, since we're waiting for a dead man to appear. Can we talk business while we wait for the second coming?"

"Whatever floats your boat, Marco. What's your proposal?"

"I have a new employer, Mr. Cray. Mr. E. prefers to remain anonymous; however, his reach is long. He has little interest in the day to day workings of your business, nor does he want a cut of the action."

"Really, what does he want then?"

"You will keep him informed as to anything unusual that comes along. Also, from time to time, he'll ask for a favour. It must be granted instantly. Nothing more does he ask or require."

"All right, this Mr. E. seems like a more than reasonable man. What's in it for me, Marco?"

"You get to remain alive." Several guns appeared and were aimed at him and Gina. Marco didn't even flinch. He almost seemed bored with it all.

"Very funny, Marco. I'm all beside myself with amusement. However, I'm quite curious. You've always been so loyal to Stephan Krebs. What did it take to turn you?"

Marco let his shoulders slump and sighed. "It was sad really, watching it happen. Poor Stephan began to lose his grip on reality, you see. First he began to mumble, then rave. He talked about werewolves and how we needed to send the werewolves after his enemies. It wasn't long after that he began to see vampires. He became unstable and I feared for my life.

"Quite by accident I was found by Mr. E. He set me up with an identity that would convince Stephan that I'd been compromised and was beyond hope, yet would leave him feeling that I hadn't betrayed him. Once the mercenaries had finished him they came to me, and we made a swift tour of Europe tying up loose ends.

"I was then returned to New York and set up as Mr. E.'s liaison in this city. So you see, I didn't betray Stephan. He betrayed himself, or at least his mind did. I believe his mind snapped under the stress."

"Really? Werewolves and vampires? You expect me to believe this?"

"What you believe, or do not believe, is irrelevant. I've told you the truth."

It was at that moment another car approached. It stopped and Stephan Krebs stepped out. He swaggered over to Marco, a sneer on his face. "I must thank you, Mr. Cray. It didn't take you long to deliver the traitor to me."

"Actually, Stephan," said Marco, "Mr. Cray has delivered you to me. What's the matter, Stephan, you look nervous. Perhaps you've brought some of your werewolves to destroy all of us. Is that it?"

"You know they took the wolves from me, you traitorous bastard. You and that damned vampire bitch."

"Oh, you mean the woman you burned alive and who came back to life to hunt you? Is that the vampire you're talking about? What was her name? Ariel? That's what you called the poor woman you set on fire, wasn't it?"

"You know damn well that was her name," snarled Stephan, as he slapped Marco hard across the face.

Marco's blow sent Stephan to the ground hard. "Touch me again and I'll kill you with my bare hands. So, tell me, Mr. Cray, have you heard enough? It's obvious this man is mad as a hatter."

"You're right, Marco. Stephan sure has lost his grip all right. What do you want me to do with him?"

"Nothing at all. My people will take good care of him, don't worry. Now, about that proposal."

"Marco, my old friend, you don't actually believe I'd fall for that crap, do you? No, I got lucky tonight. I've got both you and Stephan Krebs. Once you're both dead and I can prove it, I'll be set. I can't actually believe you came here tonight without any back up."

"Who says I did?" Marco pointed at Cray's bodyguard and the man sprouted a new hole in his forehead then crumpled to the ground.

Cray watched the man fall then freaked. "Kill them. Kill them now," he screamed. All hell broke loose. His men began to fire at Marco and Gina, then began to fall as the snipers opened fire.

Anticipating the gunfire, Marco leaped at Cray and grabbed him to use for a shield. Gina moved on the remaining gunmen as they tried and failed to get a shot at the snipers who were dropping them like flies. Soon she was among them, tossing them out into the line of fire from above.

As the battle raged Stephan Krebs made a run for safety. He had caught a glimpse of Gudrun as she charged into the battle towards him. Rounding the corner of the building he ran right into the arms of Terry Sawchuk. Stephan had only a moment to realize what had happened before those powerful arms encircled his neck and twisted savagely. There was a loud crack as his neck broke. Gudrun arrived in time to see him sink to the ground.

"Sorry, Blondie, but I wasn't taking any chances on this guy slipping away again."

"No, you did right, Terry my love. It was well done." She kissed him deeply then turned back towards the battle.

Terry was stunned for a moment then he grabbed her arm and spun her around to face him again. "Blondie?"

"If you don't stop calling me that I swear I'll bite you. I will not go through the next sixty years of my life with my husband shouting, 'Blondie.'"

Terry searched her eyes. "Gudrun, what did you...?"

"You heard me right, sweetheart. You heard me right."

Terry pulled her tight to him and hugged her fiercely. "I swear I'll never call you Blondie again."

"I don't like Goldie either."

"Damn."

"Come on, you fool. We have more work to do this night." She took his hand and led him back towards the battle. It was all over.

Most of Cray's men were dead or wounded, their weapons on the ground in a pile, and the snipers had shown themselves. Marco shoved his captive towards his fallen men. "Now then, Mr. Cray, about Mr. E.'s proposal."

"Fine, fine, Marco. Tell Mr. E. his proposal is accepted and more than generous."

"Very well." Marco winked at Terry as he dragged the body of Stephan Krebs back and dropped it beside Cray's fallen men. "We'll just let you dispose of that for us. Consider it one of the favours you owe Mr. E."

"Sure, sure, Marco. No problem. We'll deal with it."

"All right then. This concludes our business for today, Mr. Cray. I'll be in touch from time to time."

"Sure, sure, Marco. Any time at all." He was still babbling as Marco returned to his car where Gina opened the back door for him then got in and drove away. As the car disappeared he looked around, but the troop of mercenaries had vanished also.

TWO HOURS LATER, THEY'D reassembled in the royal meeting room, Harald's Great Hall as he called it.

"All right, people. Report. Marco, you first."

"Yes, Sire. As directed I contacted the local underworld leader and set up a meeting. With the aid of Miss Gudrun and her people it went better than I could have hoped.

"As we suspected it was a trap, but we managed to turn that back on them. As a bonus, Stephan himself showed up. When the dust settled, Stephan was dead, over half the local's bodyguards were dead, and Mr. Cray believes himself to be working for the mysterious and deadly Mr. E. He will keep an eye on things for us and will do us favours from time to time, whatever we ask. I'll be the liaison between you as you requested."

"Well done, Marco, you too, Gudrun. Now, are we certain Stephan Krebs is dead?"

"We are," said Gudrun. "My husband made short work of him."

"Husband? Terry?"

"Yes, Sire. It seems I'm a married man now."

"Indeed? Gudrun, are you certain?"

"I'm sure, Harald. You know me well enough to know I wouldn't do this lightly."

"Then I'm pleased for you both, we all are." This brought a round of cheers and agreement from those assembled, embarrassing both Terry and Gudrun who stepped closer to snuggle into his arms. "Marco, you've proven your worth this night. I'm pleased with you as well. Relax Gina, you're off the hook. Just keep Marco away from the wolves as much as possible to keep peace in the family.

"Peter, I leave it to you to contact Illya and inform him Krebs has finally been dealt with.

"That's it people, we can put this adventure to rest. All's well that ends well."

As the royal couple walked out arm in arm Sally spoke. "Harald, do you really believe this is over?"

"No, my darling Sally, it'll never be over. It would've been hard enough to keep eight vampires secret. Now we have eight vampires and two dozen werewolves to hide. Worse yet, the werewolves want to mate with humans to increase their number again."

"So, what's wrong with mating with a human? I'm a human."

"Yes you are, dear, and a very special human at that. However, the more werewolves there are running loose the harder it'll be to keep them hidden."

"And what if there were more of us, vampires I mean?"

"Sally, my beloved, I've explained that I'm no longer able to give you children."

"Yes, I know, but I still get broody. Like tonight, I'm feeling broody. I think you should take me home and do your kingly duty."

"Yes dear," grinned Harald. "I shall endeavour to rise to the task."

"See that you do," laughed Sally, bushing as she heard the laughter behind them from the hall.

The End

AUTHOR'S NOTE: THE king was right, it wasn't actually over. Things were quite peaceful for a time, then it all went to hell, as life so often does. In this next adventure we meet the librarian, and a most unusual one is he. It all begins with a single drop of blood ...

Vampire's Lair
Third Book in the Children of the Wild Series
by
Prudence MacLeod
Copyright August/2016
All rights reserved.
(second edition.)

Blood Trail

BLOOD SLOWLY DRIPPED from the blade of the axe held tightly in her hand. Although the drops made no sound as they hit the mossy forest floor, she was keenly aware of each and every drop slipping away, watching its painfully slow descent to the ground. Each drop that fell held her transfixed as if it was the only thing in her world.

A flicking tongue licked hungry lips as another droplet fell towards the moss as though in slow motion. She fought for control, to break the maddening focus brought on by the searing need for blood. "Control, must regain control. Hungry, so hungry, burning thirst ..."

A soft voice cut through the fog in her brain. "What's your name? Think, girl, what's your name, tell me." It wasn't actually a voice, just a memory of a voice heard ages ago, but it was enough.

"Marlene," she gasped, "my name is Marlene." That did it. The rest of the world snapped back into focus.

The baying of the dog and the shouts of the men were clear to her now. Gripping the axe tightly, she ducked behind a large tree and fought the distracting scent of blood. "The damned bear can wait," she muttered, as she allowed her body to change into the vampire's killing mode. "I need to feed."

The hound was the first to reach the clearing and find the bodies of the two men. He snuffed about for a moment, then threw back his head and gave a long howl. As he lowered his head he made eye contact with the vampire. Instantly dropping to a submissive posture, he began to crawl away.

That's when the men arrived, swearing as they ran. Suddenly spotting the bodies they skidded to a halt. "Aw Jesus, it's Jimmy, I told him to wait for me. Now I gotta tell his Ma what happened to him. Go on dog, find me that damned bear. Go on, git movin.'"

The hound just whimpered and slunk farther away from the angry man. "What the hell is the matter with you? You've seen dead men before. Get after that damned bear." Still the dog didn't move. "Fine, if you won't hunt, then I've got no reason to feed you."

With a snarl on his face he leveled the shotgun at the cowering dog, but the beast was looking past him. An axe flew through the air to shatter the skull of his companion. Before he could pull the trigger he was struck from behind, and needle sharp fangs bit deeply into his neck. As he struggled helplessly in the vampire's grip, the dog fled.

Nearly mad with the blood thirst and the killing lust, Marlene forced herself to wait. That shotgun could be a problem for one so newly risen. When the man turned away to threaten the dog she hurled the axe then charged.

The force of her body slamming into him would have sent the man flying had she not gripped him tightly. Before he could utter a startled squawk her fangs bit deep, puncturing the main artery in his neck. Hot blood spurted into her greedy mouth, and she moaned with delight as she drank noisily.

The shotgun fell from feeble hands as he struggled weakly against the vampire's steely grip. The struggles lessened then stopped, but she continued to drink greedily, the blood coursing through her like the fires of life, returning her strength, her memories, and her power over them all. Still craving more, she thrust him away.

"Control, Marlene, get control of it." She was licking her lips, and her burning gaze held him transfixed. "Are there more of you?"

He tried to crawl farther away from her, but her sudden movement stopped him. She grabbed the front of his shirt and held him off his feet in the air. *"Are there more of you? More hunters?"*

That terrible voice from a distant hell demanded a response, a response he could not refuse. "No," he whimpered, "just us four."

She hurled him away then and shook herself to gain control of the killing lust. So strong. The blood thirst was so strong when first arisen, but she had to get control of it. Oddly, it was the dog's terror that did it for her. She'd always loved dogs, and her compassion for the poor beast broke through the lust for blood.

The hunter was trying to crawl away, but she turned with liquid grace and hauled him to his feet. She dragged him back beside the bodies of the three men who'd been killed with the axe. Placing the axe in his hands, she spoke in that voice from a distant hell. *"Hold this, hold it tightly. Take this axe to the police, tell them you killed these men. You fought over a woman. You're sick in your soul at what you've done and want to confess. You will never speak of me to anyone, ever. Obey me. Go!"*

Stumbling and weak from loss of blood, the man staggered away, back the way he'd come. As soon as he was out of sight Marlene allowed herself to return to human form. She gazed down at the gaping blood stained hole in her shirt created when she'd taken a shotgun blast to the chest. With a sigh she removed the ruined shirt, bra, and jacket. She'd have to bury them.

For a moment she lightly traced her freshly healed chest with long delicate fingers. Not even a scar. Her breasts gleamed in the sun as she set out along the trail. "Now to find that damned bear."

Don't miss out!

Visit the website below and you can sign up to receive emails whenever Prudence MacLeod publishes a new book. There's no charge and no obligation.

https://books2read.com/r/B-A-ZKBBB-QNDXC

BOOKS 2 READ

Connecting independent readers to independent writers.

Also by Prudence MacLeod

Children of the Goddess
Lady Blue
Fallen Angel
Lady Justice
Lady Shadow
Lady Seeker
Watcher and Warrior
Shadow Ascending

Children of the Wild
Immortal Tigress
Children of the Wolf

Forgotten Worlds
Suvi
Echo of the Past
Survivors
Ship
Fleet
Unite

IGEN
T.E.N.

Nova series
Novan Witch
Assassin of Nova
Beyond Nova
Claimstake
Red Nova

Watch for more at https://www.prudencemacleod.com/.

Telling a story is like knitting a sweater. Start with a ball of possibilities, pull out one small thread and begin. With luck and patience you will create something quite wonderful.

About the Author

On a far off windswept island Jennifer Crandall sits with her dogs and cats creating fantastic stories for all to enjoy. She publishes as JL Crandall, Prudence MacLeod, and Jenni Leigh.

Read more at https://www.prudencemacleod.com/.